filled with unexpected kindnesses and the illuminating effect of transformation. I so admire it."

—SUSANNA MOORE, author of *In the Cut* and *Miss Aluminum*

"A beautiful, sun-drenched road story . . . a novel that's in love with the idea of America, both contemporary in its concerns and deeply nostalgic, full of Edward Hopper diners and faded blue jeans."

—*The Guardian* (UK), 10 Best Debut Novelists of 2021

"Hypnotic, stylish, and cinematic, *Highway Blue* holds you captive, like a blues song or incantation."

—OLIVIA SUDJIC, author of *Asylum Road*

"I loved this book—dark, glimmering, journeying deep into modern America on a knife edge between love and dependence."

—ROSIE PRICE, author of *What Red Was*

"Gripping from start to finish, ripe with an ever-present sense of mystery and dripping with the boldness of youth."

—*Booklist*

"An undeniably talented writer."

—*Kirkus Reviews*

HIGHWAY BLUE

A NOVEL

Ailsa McFarlane

HOGARTH

London   New York

2022 Hogarth Trade Paperback Edition

Copyright © 2021 by Ailsa McFarlane

Published in the United States by Hogarth, an imprint of Random House, a division of Penguin Random House LLC, New York.

HOGARTH is a trademark of the Random House Group Limited, and the H colophon is a trademark of Penguin Random House LLC.

Originally published in hardcover in the United States by Hogarth, an imprint of Random House, a division of Penguin Random House LLC, in 2021.

LIBRARY OF CONGRESS CATALOGING- IN PUBLICATION DATA
Names: McFarlane, Ailsa, author.
Title: Highway blue: a novel / Ailsa McFarlane.
Description: First edition. | London; New York: Hogarth, [2021]
Identifiers: LCCN 2020031891 (print) | LCCN 2020031892 (ebook) |
ISBN 9780593229132 (trade paperback; acid- free paper) |
ISBN 9780593229125 (ebook)
Classification: LCC PS3613.C43957 H54 2021 (print) |
LCC PS3613.C43957 (ebook) | DDC 813/.6—dc23
LC record available at https://lccn.loc.gov/2020031891
LC ebook record available at https://lccn.loc.gov/2020031892

Printed in the United States of America on acid-free paper

randomhousebooks.com

2 4 6 8 7 5 3 1

Title-page photo: © iStockphoto.com

Book design by Dana Leigh Blanchette

This book is for my grandparents,
and for C, J, and R.

HIGHWAY BLUE

1

- - - - - -

"Anne Marie?"

"Hi, Tricia."

"Where have you been? I've been trying to get a hold of you for days."

"Nowhere. I've been out walking Mrs. da Silva's dog, I've been home. And working."

"Then pick up your phone. I thought you were dead."

"Why did you think I'd be dead?"

"I don't know. I don't really mean that. But it would be like you. Kidnapped off the beach or something . . . I don't know."

"No. Still here."

"Good. How are you doing?"

"Fine."

"Are you?"

"I'm *fine*. Jesus, Tricia."

A pause at the other end of the line, full of static and small background noises.

"I'm sorry. Just . . . Please just call me from time to time. If you need me."

"Yeah, I will, OK? Listen, let's talk tomorrow, I've got to go now."

After Tricia hung up I put the phone back on the floor and watched as the lights from the street outside crawled up the walls.

The television was on in the apartment. There was the sound of laughter and music, talking, then laughter again; someone was changing the channels.

The television was always on. It sat on the old coffee table in the corner, murmuring softly. It was their background noise and they needed it. The lights were always on too. We couldn't afford it but they always were.

I shared the apartment with these girls. There were four of them. They worked all together in a hair and nail salon a few streets away and so there were beauty magazines everywhere, women looking out from their covers with dull glazed stares, stares ringed with heavy black, full shapes of pink mouths, wings of cheekbones, smooth faces.

We were not friends. There had been a spare room on offer and so I'd taken it and moved in when Cal left and I couldn't afford the rent on our apartment. I had been so numb back then I would have moved in anywhere.

Those girls and I stayed out of each other's way. They circled around me and I circled around them. Mostly it worked.

I was at the stove, stirring a pot of soup before I went out for my bar shift. I had my back to them but I could hear them getting ready to go out to some club in Tana Beach. They talked about boys and they talked in terms of numbers, not names. They analyzed nightly totals.

They were pragmatic.

One of them got up to leave the room and she walked past me and tried to smile. Her name was Lola and sometimes she tried to smile at me in that way that was a little self-conscious but well-meaning. I think she felt some kind of obligation for us to be friends because we lived together and all the other girls were good friends except for me. I smiled back and it was insincere and forced.

After she left, the other girls began to talk about her

because they had become tired of boys now and the rule was that if one of them left the room in the apartment then that made her fair game for the others to talk about.

There was no real malice in it. It soothed them.

Outside I could see the yellow tops of palm trees, bright because of the streetlight that was underneath them. They were tall and molting thick wads of palm fibers; their leaves glowed.

Tonight it was raining hard and the rain showed yellow, too, in a globe around the palm trees, and then beyond that where there wasn't light you couldn't see any rain.

Work at the bar was long and hot and busy under the glow of the deep purple strip lights that ran along the ceiling and picked out flashes of the teeth and eyes of people leaning forward and sitting on the bar stools. Bad music played too loudly out of a speaker in one corner. The aging manager sat on a plastic chair behind the countertop in front of the door to the kitchen and smirked and made flirtatious and overfamiliar comments as he did every night, and I gave him dead smiles and thought about emptying bottles of beer over his head. Outstretched hands waved and pushed crumpled bills at me and I pulled pints and gave them out sticky-handed.

The air was sour and bad and I was tired and my head felt heavy.

Later, after I got home, I found that the girls had brought five boys back to the apartment. The boys all wore the same thing. Their hair was cut in the same way. They spoke the same, they had affected accents and sometimes the accents slipped. I saw what they were looking for, which was for us to laugh and look nice. So I laughed. They were stupid and I saw that they were stupid right away.

I was wearing my dress from work and felt it tightly round my waist. I thought, Look at my legs, put your stupid eyes on my body. I knew they did.

I kept my face smiling. Did you know that I can be smart? I'm smart when I want. What do you want? Tell me.

Around me the other girls sat, bare legs pressed together, pale hair combed up big and brittle with spray. Heavy eyes under wads of false eyelashes. They giggled and swayed their heads with the music and spilled drinks and the air smelled like cheap vodka.

"Lucy, get your elbow off me, you're so skinny— Shauna, don't you think she's skinny? Look at this!"

"So skinny—"

"We should invite Jack, let's invite Jack—"

"—you didn't see what she wore out the other week, looking like a skank—"

The boys sat in between them and smirked and watched them.

After a while one of them kissed me and I tasted alcohol in his mouth, and chewing gum.

I watched the other people in the room and I felt cold and sealed away from them.

The boy said *let's go out somewhere.*

We walked down the street outside together.

It was still raining but it was a hot rain, a hot night.

In the distance the crash of the waves boomed from the beach. Sometimes when it rains it makes the waves sound louder.

In San Padua you can never get the ocean out of your brain.

2

———

The next day I went to the house of a woman named Mrs. da Silva to walk her dog. I went there twice a week during the afternoon, before my evening shift began at the bar.

It was easy money, and Mrs. da Silva paid well.

Her house was just off Enansa Street, set back behind a tall row of palms. It was big and white and the front lawn was wide. All the houses on this street had wide front lawns. It was a slow area where rich people with kids liked to live. The sound and smell of the ocean drifted to their windows from the boulevard onto which the street fed at one end.

And the cars that drove down this street and parked outside its houses were slick and black and low. On this afternoon they were hot in the sun.

The gardener was working on Mrs. da Silva's lawn, moving slowly around the beds at its edge. He wore a white T-shirt and he was sweating so that it clung to him in places and hung down in others.

Mrs. da Silva opened the door and said, "How are you?" emptily, the way she always did, while the big dog ran out, barking and flailing drool around the front lawn.

"This dog, this dog," she said, and then called out, "Gunner! Gunner, come here! Oh, he always listened to Frank but not to me."

I called, "Gunner!" He came over and dropped a plastic chicken on the grass beside my feet. Mrs. da Silva had never liked him much, I felt. He was her late husband's dog and I don't think she had ever really wanted him. I liked him and I think he liked me. Animals didn't usually like me much. They could feel that I didn't trust them or something like that, but not him, stupid lumbering dog.

Too big for himself.

The dog and I walked down the boulevard and over the concrete under the palms onto the sand, which was hot when I took my shoes off. Here and there people were lying on brightly colored towels, and kids were running about with plastic buckets, and girls in cheap swimsuits walked in twos along the fringes of the surf, looking surreptitiously at the people they passed.

And the water lay beyond them, blue and bright in the late sun, flecked with white reflected light, the lines of surf rolling in and crumpling on the sand.

I stood watching it for a long time and tried to follow the movements of the light on the surface of the ocean.

It stayed blue on the inside of my closed eyes.

Late that night I sat on the floor in the dark beside the refrigerator, leaning back against the kitchen cupboards. The lights in the apartment were off for once and the refrigerator drone had got into my head.

There was a bottle of whiskey on the floor beside me which was almost empty.

The place was an old peeling heap, an ugly dump, with the leak in the ceiling and the spiders in the corners and the stains on the walls and the hammering pipes. Two lousy years' backdrop, two years of squalling sprawling drunks outside the window, of broken glass, of lights and wailing sirens, the sounds of the sea and late-night street laughter.

My phone buzzed in my pocket and I took it out and looked at the little blue light of its screen shining flatly on the skin of my hand. *Tricia*.

Tricia was the cousin I was raised with. She lived down

south of La Maya now, with a husband and two sons. Those kids were crazy. I had been to visit her only once and the kids had charged around the house screaming and screaming and then the older boy had bitten my arm, hard. I had had to flush it out with iodine.

I put the phone on the floor beside me and let it ring out, watching the screen. She would be sitting at home now waiting for her husband to get back from work, and the kids were probably still running around out of bed even at this hour, screaming, breaking furniture, biting things. They loved to bite things. Tricia said that one of them had bitten a neighbor's dog recently. The dog was now agoraphobic and would not go outside.

The phone kept ringing. I turned it off.

Cal was in my head tonight. He was there most nights but there were times when he was more there than others, more insistent.

It was all this bad thinking, it brought him out, made it hard to sleep.

When I married him I was nineteen and it was a burning day in the middle of August. The summer was hot and long. We had gone to a little wooden shack church down in Tana Beach. I'd worn a white sundress borrowed from a friend, and it was a little too big so one strap kept falling off my shoulder all through the ceremony, and I had seen myself in the reflection of the glass window behind the altar, standing in this dress which was slightly too big and holding these blue flowers which cost two livra from the shop on the corner, holding them a little awkwardly, and Cal standing there beside me also a little awkward and a little drunk, and I'd had the sudden urge to laugh.

Those words we said.

Even the old minister didn't sound like he believed them. One other body to have and to hold until death do us part, one sweating, swearing, beautiful, clever, lazy, apathetic bunch of cells to keep you until the bitter end. And if you said the right words you got to walk out of that little church with a piece of paper to prove it, and then one day that piece of paper would become one of the pieces of paper that they stack together and put in a box when you die, all ready to give away to your family while they fight out the scraps left around the negative space that used to contain you.

Afterward on our wedding night, buzzed with beer and adrenaline, Cal and I broke into an old house just off Tana Beach.

It was an abandoned place, I think, or at least semi-abandoned, somebody must have still owned it because there had been a For Sale sign nailed to one of the front windows for as long as I could remember, and we were walking past it arm in arm or hand in hand or whatever we used to do back then. And there was this old place and I said to Cal, "I wonder who used to live there."

He said, "Nobody for a long time." Then he said, "Some bored housewife. Some bored husband."

I looked at him. "You don't know that. Maybe they were happy."

He shrugged, said, "I posthumously wish them every happiness." And he said it and there was evening light on his face and I remember the feeling of something I used to sense in him, a rawness under the surface.

At the time I mistook it for freedom.

So Cal went over and looked up and down the street and rattled at the bolt on the door, which was old and just a kind of sliding bolt and not a real lock, and he said, "It's loose," and he said, "Shall we go in?"

And I laughed and felt a little giddy and said, "Yes, quick, yes," and he rattled about with that lock for a moment and put a plank against it and twisted and it came away from the wood of the frame, and the door swung open and he disappeared inside.

I followed him.

The place stank of must and dust. It was dark apart from a few long red slit shapes which were made by the last of the setting sunlight coming in through the gaps between window boards, and there was sand everywhere which must have come in over the years and heaped up in drifts, heaped up against the walls and the staircase and all the furniture.

Together we walked through old rooms full of red and dark.

Outside the sun went down into the sea.

Much later after it was completely gone we sat in the deep seat of an upstairs window and looked out over the ocean which was navy and the full night sky and the heavy moon which sat copper between the two, and the air was thick with the smell of old dust and the sounds of the settling house and the old roar of the waves.

I ran my fingertips over Cal's hands and found the ridges of calluses over the tops of his palms and on the inside of his fingers, and found the small creases on the ball of his thumb and his bitten nails.

His hands were warm and dry and his skin was paper.

He left me a year after we married, a year to the day.

I woke up one morning and he wasn't there. He wasn't in bed. His jeans weren't on the floor and his coat wasn't on the door, but that was normal. At first I wasn't worried. I thought he had gone down to the beach to smoke and watch the sun come up because he sometimes did that, and he always did it alone. He would leave the room and close the door behind him without making a sound and then come back an hour or so later and the cold on his skin would wake me in the hazed-out light after dawn.

Or he had gone to buy fried fish for breakfast from the stall on the street corner by the beach. I thought he would come back within the hour, and I sat on the end of the bed and watched the wall clock, and it got later and I had to go to work, and at work they saw that something was off and said *everything all right, Anne Marie,* and I said *yes.* And I held the empty cold somewhere away from my body, held it on the edge of my mind and didn't let it in yet because he might still come back, I might still go home at the day's end and find him there smelling of salt water and sweat, which were the things he smelled of.

And I didn't.

I came home and he wasn't there.

He had left almost all of his clothes behind and so one afternoon I went down to the beach and put them in an oil drum and burned them because someone had told me to do it. I think they had got the idea from a film or something; it was a concept much touted in pop culture. They said they had done it themselves once and it had made them feel better. It didn't make me feel better. I watched the light die on the ocean through greasy black smog and got drunk and fell asleep on the sand.

Bent and broken pit of a man.

Cal. Jesus.

For a long time after he left I could remember his hands better than I could remember his face.

I leaned back against the kitchen cupboards and sank down into the smoke.

3

_ _ _ _ _ _

I woke to the sounds of an argument coming from down-stairs. I could hear everything that happened in the building, upstairs, downstairs, because the walls and the windows and doors were all so thin. You could probably put your hand through them if you wanted to. Sometimes I thought about doing that.

The voices were dim because I was half dreaming still and so the sounds became part of my dream.

Then I woke up.

There was an empty takeout carton on the floor and the room smelled bad.

I went to open the window and put my head out and looked down to the ground floor and there standing beside the main entrance was Mr. Weiss who lived down-stairs.

Once a week or so his wife threw him out and told him she was leaving him, and when that happened he would stand outside on the pavement and for a couple of hours the arguing would continue and she would lean out of the window to shout at him, and after a while of that his tone would become contrite and wheedling and she would let him back in.

He was saying, "Come on, baby, take me back. I didn't mean it, I swear."

She, above him, yelled indeterminately.

I shut the window.

The clock on the wall said it was gone half past three in the afternoon. I hadn't slept till almost dawn the night before, and when I finally did it had been broken, fitful, colored with unsettling dreams of fractured and half-remembered faces that slipped away quickly from my wak-ing brain as I tried to get a clear sight of them. There was an odd ringing whine in my head and I pressed my hands against my eyes and small red lights moved about inside my eyelids.

My body felt old and tired, my head thick. In the bath-room I splashed cold water on my cheeks. It didn't do any-thing. I stood, hands gripping either side of the sink, looking at my face in the mirror, watching the slow movement of water droplets sliding down my forehead. I looked exhausted and small and pale. The twin points of my shoulders showed under my shirt. Everything about me seemed for a strange moment to have shrunk in on itself, and I felt that I was held by my own eyes in the mirror.

After a second I shook my head and turned away.

The kitchen cupboard was empty and that meant that I would have to go and buy food from somewhere, or maybe later I could stop by the bar although it was my evening off and they would have leftovers because they often did toward the end of the week, and maybe there would be French toast or some pancakes today and maybe I could take a little cream from the fridge because I was friendly with the chef.

The apartment was empty now because the girls were all out at work, and I wandered inside it with nowhere to go, moving the dirty plates on the sideboard into the sink and turning on the tap without any intention of cleaning them and turning it off again; tuning the old radio on the windowsill in and out of static and watching the people and cars moving about the hot loud street under the window and splashing tap water listlessly on my face, and drinking yesterday's cold coffee from a cup on the table.

Tuning in the radio, tuning it out again.

It began to grow dark and I thought I would go out and

walk down to the ocean and look at the lights on the water. I wanted badly to be out of the apartment and not to look at the old plates in the sink and smell the old coffee and feel the walls close on all sides.

I locked the apartment behind me.

Downstairs at the front doors of the building was the shape of somebody behind the frosted glass. I paused and then opened the door and stepped from the dark hallway into the street light outside.

My husband, Cal, was standing on the pavement.

4

- - - - - - -

We sat facing each other at a table in a bar. It was early evening and our drinks were in front of us, untouched.

He was wearing a shirt, a white shirt, and his hair was shorter, it wasn't long anymore. His phone was on the table. It had a long fracture running down the screen and I followed the lines of the break with my eyes.

I said, "You've changed a lot."

A banality, of course he had, over two years had passed since I last saw him.

New shirt and no more tangle of long hair on his shoulders.

Cal was always shifting, that was how he was. Shifting ideas, shifting plans, always going somewhere, always something on his mind, the next thing. With each new idea that hit him he used to spend days in a peak of faddish energy and then soon after it would all be gone and he'd slump down into apathy again.

Until the next one.

Maybe he had made one of them stick.

It wasn't impossible, he knew how to carry himself, he could make people like him.

They often judged him by his looks and underestimated how clever he was and he turned that to his advantage. We used to go out to bars and parties and there were always other girls around him. He was good with them. He was good at talking.

He said, "I worked at a company for a while. A friend's company."

I raised my eyebrows. I said, "Was it legal?"

"Of course. What do you think I would do?"

"Rob people blind. Rob blind people. Something like that."

He said, "It was a car repair shop."

I couldn't read his expression. Strange that I used to know the ins and outs of that face completely.

After a moment he said, "So how have you been? You seem good. You're happy?"

I said, "It's been almost two years, Cal."

"I know."

"How did you find me?"

"I went to visit old Irvine. He told me where your place was. I knew you'd still be in San Padua. I didn't think you would have gone far from Tana Beach."

"Why, you didn't think I could make it?"

He gave a half shrug.

I stared at his face. Cutting his hair had changed it so much. "Where did you go, Cal?"

He was quiet for a moment. Then he said, "North. Costa Maria."

"That's not what I meant."

He stared down at the zinc tabletop. He was tapping against it with the nails of one hand. They were short and bitten; around them there were ragged edges of skin.

I said, "Why have you come back?"

He shrugged. "I missed you. I've been thinking about you."

"Don't lie."

"Anne Marie—"

He looked at me and his mouth worked a little and there was an expression on his face which was something unknowable, and he said, "I'm not lying." His voice caught a little. "Jesus."

"What?"

"You've changed so much. You didn't use to be like this."

I drew in my breath. "It's been a long time."

He looked at me and it was an odd look with something behind it that I couldn't get a hold of. At the table behind us a young couple were kissing, their drinks untouched in front of them. Their presence seemed obtrusive, they made me self-conscious. I tried to ignore them. Instead I watched the tap-tapping of Cal's fingernails on the tabletop. The little show of plastic beneath the cuff of his shirt.

I said, "Nice watch."

"Thanks."

"Never knew you to wear one."

He put one hand over his eyes and held his fingers against his closed lids, then he leaned forward across the table.

I said, "What happened to this job you had?"

He drew in a breath and paused; his face worked. After a moment he said, "Listen, Anne Marie. I owe money."

"You shit, I knew it."

"I'm sorry. I am sorry. I had nowhere else to go."

"Try some rich banker's wife up in the Heights. Someone who can buy you nice things. Always worked for you before."

"Anne Marie. I'm sorry. I'm sorry, all right? What do you want me to do? What do you want me to say? I did what I did, that's past. I can't take it back. But I have nothing." For a second his voice broke a little and he stopped, and I saw that he was sweating slightly in the bluish lights which came down from the ceiling. "I have nothing left."

Suddenly he put his hand in his pocket and frantically rummaged. "I still have my wedding ring," he said. "I still have it, look, here. I can put this back on."

"Get out, Cal."

"No, look, there, it's back on, that's for you." He took hold of both of my hands, tightly. He said, "You have to help me. Anne Marie."

He said, "If you don't I'm done."

"God, Cal." I pulled my hands out of his. "Even if I wanted you bringing whatever stinking little thing you have going here onto my door, even if I wanted that, you think I have anything to give you? I have nothing. *Nothing*. I can't help you."

He slumped in his seat. He said, "Jesus. Jesus."

"You must have known there was nothing I could do."

He laughed bleakly and said, "Worth a shot."

I stood up. I said, "I'm sorry. I'm going home."

"Wait. Don't leave already."

"Why not?"

"Stay, finish the drinks. We could get a bite. Talk."

"I don't know what I would say to you."

He rubbed his eyes and then just for a moment smiled crookedly; a hint of the old Cal in that smile, the old self-assurance. "Come on, Anne Marie. After all, we did marry each other."

"A long time ago. I must have been so far out of my mind . . ."

"You were. I was. I liked that in you."

I stared at him. Then I snorted. I said, "I'm going to go home, Cal."

I stood and picked my bag up from the floor and put on my coat.

He said, "Come on. Wait."

"I'm going home."

"Fine. I'll walk you back."

There was an assurance in his manner again, but it was a false assurance, hollow, and just for a moment it had slipped and shown weakness behind it.

"I don't need you to."

"I want to. Come on, let me walk you home. You're in Tana Beach. I'm staying near there. We're going the same way."

"Whatever. Walk me back if it helps you."

As we left, the barman called after us, "Have a good evening," and it made me look back to reply to him, and as I glanced back from the doorway I saw the little room of the bar like a play in a box full of orange light, and little people sitting at the tables all held up in conversations, and pictures on the walls and rows of bottles behind the counter, green and orange, all of it held in this little puppet-box room, this theater light-box, and just for a flash I felt very huge and nothing in that room seemed real.

Cal said, "You all right? What's wrong?"

I shook my head and said, "Nothing."

We walked down the floodlit boulevard outside, where palm trees made strange talon shadows out of the dark.

Somewhere to our left was the faint rush of the sea.

The houses in this part of town stood up on stilts and their old wooden faces sagged down into the street, shutters hanging off at angles, old green paint bubbled and peeling.

Every now and again we passed the sack-shapes of people lying on the ground, sleeping on pieces of cardboard.

Cal was quiet as we walked. After a while he said, "I never missed this."

"What?"

"This place. This stinking town. Everything just waiting to fall into the dust. Waiting to suck the life out of you till you crawl down to the ocean to wither up on the beach."

His face in the streetlights was hard.

"Doesn't sound like you were doing much better up north."

He gave a harsh laugh. "You're right there."

"What was it like? Where you went."

He shrugged. "Not so different. Colder. Different houses. Different people."

I nodded. In the back of my mind were old habits that wanted me to walk close beside him with my arm around the slack movement of his waist.

I pushed them down.

And there was silence between us again. Somewhere down the street, far away, a drunk was singing: discordant, wandering, a few disjointed bars tailing off and hanging in the air.

Up ahead was the opening of a little alley which led away from the oceanfront. It was a shortcut through the block of houses to the other side of Tana Beach, and we always used to walk down it together when we went to the water at night.

Cal said, "Let's take the cut-through."

We walked into the dark away from the streetlights. Around us the hulks of piled garbage bags showed deeper black.

Cal began to whistle and the sound fell flatly on the blank house walls.

I said, "Don't do that."

"What?"

"The whistling. I don't like it."

. . . set out running but I'll take my time, a friend of the Devil is a friend of mine . . .

And I turned to look back at the singing drunk and all of a sudden someone stepped out from the alley wall and stood between the two of us and the road back to the ocean. He was very tall and broad. The top half of his face was in shadow and I stared into the wide whites of his eyes and the great yawns of his pupils in the pit of those eyes.

He filled almost the whole width of the alley and blocked out the far streetlights.

"Where's the money, Cal?"

There was something in his hand which was a dark shape and I saw that it was a gun.

I said, "Jesus, Cal, oh God—"

I couldn't move and my breath was hot and tight in my throat.

Cal said, "Stay still, Anne Marie, don't move—"

There was a taste of metal in my mouth.

Outside, any sound now seemed a long way off.

The man said, "Come on, where is it?" and he made a jerking motion with his hand which I saw was shaking a little.

Jesus.

I thought, I am going to die.

Right now this moment today I am going to die in this stinking alley.

Jesus Christ.

Cal stretched out his hands. He said, "Don't do anything—come on—just calm down, calm down."

"Shut up."

"I don't have what you want but there's some money in the wallet, there, take it, there's my watch, my phone—"

I half saw out of the corner of my eye the dark motions of Cal fumbling in pockets. Something was thrown on the ground.

The man said, "Her too."

And I said, "I don't have anything."

And he said, "Shut up, you too—money on the floor—"

And then he raised his arm and I saw Cal lunge to one side toward him and push him to the ground and the two together fell into me and a loud sharp sound cracked out in the alley and something like an elbow came down hard and hit me in the face and knocked my head against concrete and I gasped and my head was ringing my ears buzzing and something hard was against the back of my hand that was maybe metal and I cried out and a hand closed around my ankle and pulled me sharply to the ground and he was there holding on to my leg and his arm was raised and he was going to bring it down on me hard and then from somewhere the gun went off.

For a moment, echoes bounced.

The shape of him lurched backward and his hand came off me and his body slumped on my leg.

I felt something hot all over me, slick and sticky on my hands.

My stomach heaved.

I threw up in the alley and I heard it hit the ground and some of it hit my leg.

There was the sound of Cal's voice and he was saying, "Oh, Jesus, Jesus—" His hand was on the back of my neck, on the back of my shirt.

He grabbed at my arms and shook me. He said, "Anne Marie, we have to go right now."

He pulled his hand away. He said, "God. There's blood on you."

I looked down at myself. Something smelled, there was a smell, I didn't know of what, salt, metal, bile.

My arms and legs felt leaden and I couldn't move and there was a ringing whine in my ears.

He said, "We have to go right now—"

"I can't, I can't—"

"You can."

"I can't move—"

"You have to. Come on, come on, you have to. Any second someone's going to be here and they're going to call the police and you're going to jail, we're both going to jail. We're done if you don't move right now—"

"Help me. Help me—"

He put his hand under my arm and my body sagged on him and we walked like that, staggering, and he said, "Is there anyone in your apartment?" I stared at his face in the dark and he shook me. "Come on, Anne Marie, is there anyone home in your apartment?"

"No—I don't think so—no. They'll be out, it's Saturday."

"Good. We need to get in there and change your clothes. We've got to get out of San Padua tonight."

I pressed my hand against my eyes. "All right. All right . . ."

"Come on. Good girl."

The lights were off in the apartment when we got there. A stack of plates were in the sink. Faintly there was the smell of cheap hairspray in the air.

I said, "There's no one here."

"Get a trash bag. We have to get rid of these clothes. Don't turn the light on."

In the bathroom I ran hot water in the basin and put my hands in it and there was the smell, cutting, sharp, somehow wet.

I threw up in the toilet again.

Through the door Cal said, "Come on, come on, you're OK." He was outside in the hallway and he was putting a trash bag with my clothes in it down the rubbish chute. I could hear the plastic rustling.

I switched on the bathroom light.

My face in the bathroom mirror above the sink loomed in front of me, white and gray. My pupils were huge.

There were dark red streaks on my forearms and clinging congealed bits. The sink water was pale pinkish. There was red on my legs too where he had fallen on them.

Cal said, "Can I come in?"

He stood in the doorway. He stared at me and he seemed caught. "Christ," he said hoarsely.

I put my hands on the sides of the basin and held on to it. My arms were shaking and I couldn't make them stop.

He came over and put my hands in the water and rubbed at them again and again.

I stared at the water. I stared at its movement and watched it change color.

There were little flaring swirls of red scraps swimming around in it.

I went into my room and put on clean clothes, all with the lights out because it felt better in the dark. It felt like I should be moving in the dark. I put clothes in an old rucksack. It was the rucksack I had brought when I first moved here.

And I thought, I can't come back here ever again.

There was nothing I loved enough to take with me but I thought I should have something, so I took a little blue chipped porcelain elephant that I kept on the bedside because it had belonged to my great-aunt Delphine and she had given it to me once a long time ago. Its face was ugly. It had gold flecks on its back. She had bought it from a market specially to give to me when I was little, that one for me and a red one for Tricia. The paint had probably given me mercury poisoning or something.

Cal said, "Take blankets. Take food, any money."

In the kitchen cupboards there were cans of beans and a loaf of bread and a packet of cookies which was half-empty and there was a block of cheese and a bottle of vodka.

"Is this all you have?"

"Yeah."

"All right. All right. It gets us somewhere. Come on. We should get going."

Outside in the pool of orange light under a streetlamp I stopped.

I said, "Cal. I can't."

"What? Come on, babe, yes you can. Come on. Anne Marie. If we get up onto the main highway we can get a ride and be out of here by morning."

My legs were shaking. I hadn't noticed them shaking until now and when I noticed I wondered how I hadn't before. They knocked against each other.

My mouth tasted of vomit.

I said, "Oh God, Cal."

And he said, "Come on, not now, we can't go there now. Time for that later. Right now we have to get out. The police are going to be all over that soon and they maybe already are. Come on, babe, come on, just keep with me. Do what I do. If we can get a ride on the main highway we can get down to La Maya by tomorrow. I have a friend there. He can put us up. We can stay with him a day or two. Get this figured out. Anne Marie."

He took hold of both my hands. I looked up at his face under the streetlights. I couldn't see his eyes and they were in blots of dark, they were in a double blot of dark that sat across his face.

He pressed my hands tight.

He said, "Come on, up to the highway."

I took a shaking breath.

I said, "Jesus—OK—OK."

We walked upward toward Pine Hills where the highway ran through. Exhaustion ran deep in me, starting down in the pit of my stomach. My feet were heavy.

And I kept smelling that smell, that wet metal smell, and I didn't know whether it was on me and real or whether it was in my head.

At the top of the rise we came out at the back of the houses of Pine Hills, a few low bungalows, scrubby little pieces of garden full of rusting metal. No streetlights here but up ahead the line of lights that was the La Maya highway.

Somewhere off in the distance a dog barked.

In front of us across the road rose the banking of Munina Mountain and it was hulked up and sliding away darkly into stars and darker blots of cloud.

I turned.

Out on our other side the city of San Padua fell away to the ocean in tiers of orange and yellow lights and they were strung out in irregular lines and straggling and winding, and the tiny movements of cars were twin points of red, and here and there flashings of blue, and the faint sounds of police sirens drifting, and above that the sighing of the ocean.

On the horizon the first slick of pale light was beginning to appear.

It felt like a long time that we stood on that rise, thumbs out, waiting for someone to pick us up.

My head ached sickeningly.

We must have looked rough, exhausted, bruising on my face, old rucksack on my back.

It was a hot night but I was cold. And it was a cold that seemed like a new, deeper kind.

Cal put a blanket around my shoulders. Mutely I watched him. His face seemed a long way away.

After about half an hour someone stopped.

An old red van pulled over onto the dust in front of us. There were dark rust flecks and sprays of mud around the wheel wells. The driver was a man in his fifties. He was balding but he still had a little long blondish hair and it was pulled into a ponytail at the back of his head.

Beside him in the passenger seat there was a woman. Her hair was dry and brown and her eyes sat in deep folds.

A bead necklace hung from the rearview mirror. There was a small painted figurine on the dashboard beneath it and the figure had six arms and a tall crown and one leg was raised up, dancing, some sort of goddess.

The man said, "Where are you headed?"

"La Maya," said Cal.

"We're going as far as Otto, so we can drop you there if that's a help. I'm Jem. This is Tulip."

"I'm Cal."

"Anne Marie."

"Nice to meet you both. Jump in the back. Pull the side door—there you go."

We got in and the van began to move.

Inside the enclosed space in the back there was dark and swaying motion. It smelled strongly of incense, something like patchouli. It made me carsick.

Over the seat partition Jem said, "Early hour for you both to be traveling."

"Sickness in the family," Cal said. "My wife's people are down in La Maya. We heard this morning. Got to get down there as fast as we can."

Cal was good at lying. He didn't have to think.

"Sorry to hear that."

"Thanks, we appreciate it."

"It happens."

"Yeah."

There was some sort of pile of rugs and cushions behind us and I crawled over to it and lay back, my head against the far wall.

I was rocked with the motion of the van and stared out of the back window at the huddled stain of light that was San Padua.

I watched it become small.

At some point I must have fallen asleep and I dreamed I was running but my legs were moving very slowly. I tried with everything in me but I couldn't make them go faster.

There was something behind me, I knew it.

My body was full of fear so that I couldn't breathe with it. It made me choke but my legs wouldn't go faster.

The air was thick as if it had become water.

When I woke I was damp with sweat and my shirt stuck to my underarms.

Out of the window the sun was coming up and the sky was streaked red and blood-orange.

Jem said, "Look at that."

Tulip said, "Beautiful."

Jem said, "You both awake back there? Reckon you drifted off for a little while."

Cal laughed. He said, "Long night."

"I bet. We're coming up toward the town. Shouldn't be too long before we're there; half an hour or so."

Cal said, "Thanks. What takes you both to Otto, by the way? You from here?"

Jem said, "No, our place is up north. Close to Costa Maria. You know it?"

"It's something special up there," said Tulip.

"Yeah," said Jem. "We've got a place. It's a farm. Grow some herbs and things. Some vegetables. Got a horse off Tulip's people last year and there's some goats, chickens, stuff like that. We take the wool from the goats and we dye it. That's what you see in those, those bags back there. We sell some of it off in Otto every now and again. More of a hobby than money, you know. We like to go down early so we drive through the night and then there's all day to do what we like with when we get there. Time to go and have some food, time to walk around a bit. It's not a bad town. We like it."

Tulip said, "We like the empty roads when it's late."

The van drove down the winding coast road over the summit of a ridge toward the town, with the light of the early sun in the sky and the sea flooding out to our right-hand side. The little houses in white and red were clustered small against the foldings of the foothills, their windows catching points of light and the highway picked out and cutting into the scrubby hillside, snaking downward.

The ocean bounced with sparks of morning sun.

Along the coast long lines of waves rolled in and wrapped white and foaming around the point.

Jem said, "Look at that. What a morning. What a morning."

There was nobody about in the town yet and all the shops and cafes were closed up and their doors covered by iron grilles and their awnings rolled up and their chairs and tables stacked outside.

Jem and Tulip pulled up in the deserted main square for us to get out.

Cal said, "Good luck with your wool."

"Thanks. You'll have to remember us if you come up to Costa Maria."

"We will."

"Take care."

"You too."

The town of Otto was a small place. It brought in wealthy people from up north for vacations in the sun, and they came streaming down the coastal highway during the peak of the summer season to park their expensive cars up in lots beside the beach and expose their skin to the sun. There were expensive houses here and beachfront hotels with verandas and closed red umbrellas and big glass-covered entranceways, and potted palm trees and flowers.

But the rich tourists wouldn't be here until later in the year. For now the town was still and dewy in milk pale light, everything silent apart from the rush of the surf. Daylight was breaking fully now over the ocean and we sat on the concrete boulevard and looked out over the water and we ate dry cookies from the packet we had brought with us. They were all broken up. I had lain on them when I was lying on my rucksack in the back of the van.

Eating something helped a little.

We sat in silence and watched the waves.

After a while the first early-morning walkers began to appear.

There was an old man and an old woman and a dog and the dog was very fat and short-legged and walked on a leash and the old man and old woman were also fat and short-legged and the three of them moved slowly along the boulevard.

I said, "How far to La Maya from here? An hour or so?"

"About that."

I nodded.

Then I said blankly, "Do you think they've found him yet?"

"Yeah."

Down on the sand of the beach below us a gull pulled at a fish carcass; I stared at it.

Cal said, "Do you know which of us made it go off? The gun."

The gull tugged at a long stretch of skin. Its beak stabbed sharply.

I said, "No."

"Jesus."

"I suppose it doesn't matter."

"No. I suppose it doesn't."

"Doesn't change it."

"No."

After a moment Cal got up and began to walk toward the main road.

I looked after him and he was moving away contained in his body and for a second I felt lost down a tunnel.

He stopped and looked back at me and he said, "Coming?"

"Yeah."

I got up and followed him and we walked out toward the edge of town and the highway.

5

- - - - - -

My mother once took me on a trip.

I was a little kid and I think I must have been five years old or something close to it because I had just finished my first year of school, and it was right at the beginning of the summer vacation and my mother said, "We're going on a trip."

There was this old car that we had which I think was a blue car and she had packed it with some things like blankets and soft toys and she had made a sort of nest in the passenger seat for me, I remember, and there was a small pink dolphin on a chain which hung down from the rearview mirror and it moved and caught the light as we drove and my mother said *don't play with that* and so I did and I kept reaching for it, reaching up while she was driving which must have been distracting for her and she kept saying *no*, and sometimes as we drove I said *can I go to the bathroom* and I have memories of waiting in a long line for the bathroom somewhere in some service station with a hand holding mine, which was my mother's hand, but I have no memories of the body attached to it. I have a vague impression of a distant face.

I think she took that vacation because she thought she should and because she thought that maybe I would remember it forever and that maybe it would become a treasured memory, a sort of last-ditch attempt to give me one of those, because I don't remember other trips after that one.

Anyway.

All I can remember of it now is waiting in line for the bathroom.

We got a lift down to La Maya with an almond salesman.

He picked us up almost right away. He was short and his hair was buzzed and he wore a green shirt which said *Thompson Growers* on it.

He had a truck full of almonds that he was taking from the north, where they had been grown in an almond field, to the south, where there was no way to grow almonds anymore.

He said there was no way to grow almonds there now because the climate had changed in the last ten years.

Once they had grown almonds and oranges and lots of other things in the south. Now they couldn't because the weather was volatile and the wet seasons down there had become too wet so that all that could be grown were things that liked the wet a lot, which was mainly alligators.

Once he got to the south the almond salesman's almonds would be made into almond cookies in a factory owned by one of the largest cookie-manufacturing companies in the nation.

The company was called Leo Fitz Confectionery Company.

They had an emblem which was a kid sitting on a cookie that was flying like a magic carpet and the kid was wearing a crown and a cape.

The almond salesman said, "It's five grams of almonds per cookie. Twenty cookies to a pack. You think how many packs of cookies they make a day in that place. You think how many almonds they need. That's I don't know how many almonds. That's good for me. That's good for my business. All this climate change is good for my business. Things have worked out for us up north."

He looked at us to see if we were listening.

I gave a half smile.

He said, "I'll give you a guess how many tons of almonds I move a year."

"I don't know."

"Go on. Guess."

"I don't know."

"Then I'll tell you."

"OK."

"Fifty."

"Oh."

In La Maya there was some sort of a grassy public area beside the southern beach of the city and the almond driver dropped us near it and we walked over there to find somewhere to sleep off a few of the midday hours. It was crowded and people had strung their hammocks in small spots of shade out of the heat of the afternoon, and they had set up little smoking portable barbecues to fry sausages, and children were running around topless and shouting in high voices.

The women wore long fringed skirts in bright colors. The men wore old shorts and their tanned skin sagged.

The beach was divided from the grass by a low concrete wall and people had put out scarves along its length and were sitting on them and little kids sat in rows and dangled small skinny legs.

The water seemed too blue. Pelicans bobbed on its surface. Farther north there were no pelicans but down here they were everywhere. Their heads were tucked down into their chests so that their long beaks were hidden and every now and again they flung out their wings in a burst and ran over the water to take off, batting at the surface of the water with stupid flapping feet. Then one of them would come down to land and would careen for a few feet in a great ball of spray and the others would watch it and honk in a frenzy.

I didn't want to go down onto the beach and I hung back under the shade of the palm trees.

I said, "Someone will see us."

"Don't be paranoid. The police won't know who they're looking for. Not down here. Maybe not up there even. We put about three hundred miles behind us last night."

He turned and tried to reach for my hand.

He said, "We wait it out down here for a little while. We play it safe just in case. You have to try to at least look like you're relaxed. People are going to notice you, jumping around the way you are every five seconds."

"I'm not jumping around."

"You are. It doesn't look right. And you've got bruises on your face."

I stared at him. I said, "You're acting so casual."

"I'm not casual. But you have to pretend. Give people what they're expecting. Otherwise they'll notice you."

Then he said, "Here, I'll buy you a drink."

"I don't want a drink."

"Then I'll buy me one. You can sit and watch me drink it. Come on."

Down by the water was a bar which was a small sort of shack leaning against the wall. Its roof was sheets of corrugated iron and its walls were boards of plywood. Dried palm fronds had been stapled on to make it look like it was built from palms and some of them hung off in rough clumps and showed the plywood underneath. There was a hatch in the front with a counter and on the counter there were small racks of peanuts and potato chips and a big poster showing different types of ice cream and their prices.

A sign hung above the hatch, made from a surfboard.

On it was painted the name of the beach bar: ROSA'S BEACHSIDE REFRESHMENTS.

A woman stood in the hatch and she wore a red apron and a small red hat.

She said in a monotone, "What do you want?"

Cal said, "What drinks do you have?"

"Beer. Coke. Lemonade."

"A beer, please."

"I can't sell you the beer before twelve o'clock."

"Then why did you tell me you had it?"

"'Cause I do. You just can't buy it."

There was a pause where they stared at each other. Cal said, "Coke then."

We walked down the beach until we found a spot under a palm tree that was protected from the heat and ringed by clumps of spiked grass which stabbed at the back of my head when I lay down. The shadow patterns of the palm leaves covered the bare skin of my arms.

I closed my eyes and then there was just the soft sink and swill of the little wavelets and the yelling of the kids which seemed a long way away for some reason from down there on the ground. The tiredness made my head ache.

When I closed my eyes there were buzzing needles of light on black and flashes of electric blue and nauseous purple and I opened them again because anything was better than the sickness.

I held my hand up to my face and I could see its fine details very close, the small dry cracks full of scab around my fingernails and the little scuffed flaps in the skin and the tiny whorls of my fingerprint.

Bunches of cells, that was all it was, and that was all we were, bunches of cells. Big old bunches moving about and now and again knocking into each other, and sometimes one big bunch putting an end to the movements of another and then that one falling down on the ground and other small reconfigurations of the same basic stuff eating all its component parts and building something else, or sometimes two big bunches knocking together to make another small bunch of cells that would grow and grow and keep moving around and bumping into things until they could in their turn make another bunch of cells, who could in their turn make another, who could make another, and on and on.

To one side of me Cal was lying very close. He had fallen asleep almost right away.

I studied his face and I could see the tiny lines around his closed eyes and at the corners of his mouth, their curve and fade, an eyelash lying quivering beside his nose and moving with the in and out of his breath.

Behind me there were loud voices laughing, a party of old couples who were sitting on canvas chairs on the sand down toward the tide line. They had a red cooler beside them.

The old women wore swimsuits and sun hats and the brims of the sun hats drooped.

I listened to their conversation and drifted.

"No, that was the one before this one, now she's with Jim or Jack or what's-his-name, the one from up near Favelle."

"I always knew they wouldn't last. I knew it, didn't I say right back in January when she first started with him? I said they wouldn't last."

"You always know how to spot it, Elizabeth—she always knows—you did say it—you said it before with the last one—"

The voices drifted in and then out again.

I must have fallen asleep, because it was dark and Cal was shaking me awake. All the people around us had gone and in the distance two white car headlights were moving alongside the beach toward us.

I said, "What time is it?"

Cal said, "Dunno. Late. You slept for hours. That's a warden coming and they'll move us on. We should get moving and get you a proper bed to sleep in."

My mouth felt dry and there was a strange taste in it. I said, "Where are we going?"

"Into town, and then we'll go and see if we can get on one of those trains out to the suburbs. Stay at my friend's place for the night."

"Is that going to be all right? What if he—"

"He won't. I've known him years. He's a good friend. It'll be all right. Come on."

Up off the beach we waited at the roadside in the dark. The headlights came closer and stopped when they reached us. It was a white truck and the city badge was on the door.

The warden rolled down the window.

He wore a green cap and a green jacket and they had the city badge on them too.

He said, "No sleeping on the beach. It's not allowed. It's a city-protected area."

Cal said, "No, Officer, we're leaving. Fell asleep earlier and just woke up and now we're walking back into town. Le Roi Station."

The warden looked me up and down; he looked skeptical.

After a moment he said, "You're going into town? Jump in the back. I'll take you to the park gates. Le Roi's not far from there but it's a long way to go if you're walking."

"Appreciate it."

The inside of the truck smelled cloying. An air freshener swung from the rearview mirror, it was vanilla bean or something, and beneath that the smell of old cigarette ash and fast food. The radio murmured from the dashboard. Faint voices and static.

Through the silhouettes of palms I could see the skyline of La Maya across the bay and all the buildings were lit up in flushes of color, great washing cones of spotlight beams along the walls and all in aurora colors of green and pink. The city sounds drifted out toward us over the water through the rolled-down window of the car and there were sirens and distant music and the acceleration of motorbikes. I thought about everything that was happening over there in my line of sight, locked behind walls, all the people tucked away in boxes where living happened, the families, the people, and all of them just moving about and doing whatever it was they did with themselves, pushing on, rolling on.

There was a film my mother used to like a lot and I liked it too when I was a kid. We watched it together. It was a French film about a girl living in a city and sometimes in the film she walked up to the top of a tall building and told herself things about what was happening in the city at that moment. She liked to invent fancy stories and some of them were funny; it was a comedy. The actress had short dark hair and big dark eyes and I used to imagine her going home after working on the film every day and sitting tired in an open apartment looking over water.

And of course everybody wanted pictures of her because she was pretty and slim and she was on the TV so that people knew her face.

Anyway.

When I was sitting in that truck looking across at the lights on the other side of the water I could also see the lights of cars moving around and each car had one or two or maybe more people in it, talking together or not talking or just going about the process of getting from one place to another fast, which was part of living and deemed important.

Small lives, like my own small life.

At the park gate we got out and the warden got out too and came around to the passenger door and said he would help me out.

He said, "That's a nasty bruise on your face there, sweet."

"I had a fall," I said.

He looked at Cal for a long moment. "You her boyfriend?"

I looked sharply at him.

Cal said, "Yeah."

He said it easily. He was casual. He was very good at lying.

"Might want to get that looked at. You never know with a knock to the head."

I said, "Really, I'm fine."

"How old are you anyway, sweet?" He was looking at me now and his look was intent.

I stared at him, swallowed.

I thought, Stop asking me things. I was not good at lying. "Twenty-one."

He looked at Cal, who said, "We should be going. Got a train to make out to the other side of town."

The warden opened his mouth, then he paused and closed it. He was still looking at Cal but after a moment he got back in the truck and started the engine.

From the open window he leaned out and said, "You take care. Get that bruise looked at."

He was looking at me when he drove away.

I watched the lights of the truck fall back into the dark of the beach peninsula. In front of us on the other side of the gate was a long street and it was bright and residential and divided suddenly from the night of the park and the beach.

A few cats skulked about in the shadows under the parked cars.

I said, "How long will it take for the bruise to go down?"

"I don't know. A week. Maybe a few. It's big."

"He thought you gave it to me."

"I know."

6

Here is something about Cal.

He was born up north near Costa Maria and he had three brothers and from what he told me his family was a nice family, which is to say a normal family who never did anything overtly strange to him, and who lived in a small house on the edge of the city with a couple of dogs. The dogs were too big for the house.

Cal's father worked in a factory which made car engines and that factory was a half hour's metro ride from the family home.

His job in the engine factory was to put a piece of tape over the flaps of the cardboard boxes that were used to hold the engine parts, one piece of tape per box, so that he worked all day and never once saw the parts themselves.

He put on the tape and sent them off and then went home every evening and Cal's mother made him dinner and sometimes he shouted at the boys and sometimes he just went to bed, and then the next day he went into work and did the same thing again.

Cal talked about his father the way I talked about my mother.

The year I first met Cal he had a place at the back of Tana Beach and he lived there with a man and a woman who were old friends, although I never found out how they came to know each other. The man's name was Ruby and the woman's name was Sam.

Ruby was a nickname. I have no idea what he was really called and neither did anybody else. He always seemed hazed out.

Sam was sometimes his girlfriend and sometimes not, and I think maybe at some point she and Cal had been something too. She had dryish yellow hair and a ring through her lip and brown eyes which were always drawn around with kohl and she wore old faded T-shirts and little tiny skirts and black tights full of holes. And she sat lolling about stoned in that place all day.

The first time I met her she walked up to me and took hold of both my hands and kissed me on the lips very hard and smiled and Cal laughed and said, "Sam is friendly," and to me it seemed a little like an act and something done to shock but anyway I laughed too and then after that she liked me.

That place was two rooms and one of them was Ruby and Sam's and the other was the main room which had a sort of cramped little kitchenette on one side and French windows and half a barrel with a cushion on top to sit on and in one corner a sofa bed which was Cal's.

In the hot evenings we sat all together on the sofa bed and ate off bowls on our knees. The air was all slow-curling smoke and the curtains of the French windows lifted and hung in the small breeze off the ocean, and everything was held deep and warm in the red light from the lamp. Cal had his quick talking and humor and sudden shifts between warmth and harshness, and the flash of a sharp twisted smile. He called me beautiful and his skin tasted of the hot salt of his sweat. And I was caught, I was caught in all of it and floating in happy looseness, and for the first time in my life it didn't feel like I was suffocating.

After about three weeks of knowing Cal I had already moved in with him.

I remember it now, indistinct and dark and swimming through smoke, a dream in red haze.

- - -

There were still a few people sitting on the waiting chairs outside the little metro station when we got there. Mosquitoes danced around the lights up on the roof and buffeted against the glass. Those mosquitoes were everywhere. La Maya had swampy land at its outskirts and they bred there out in the soupiness and then swarmed in toward the houses and the lights and the people. They needed ready supplies of blood to drink. I could feel them landing on me, the sharp moments of their bites.

An old man was slumped on the ground beside the ticket machine and he wore a patterned shawl around his shoulders and his head was tipped forward. Beside him a small white dog was sleeping. In front of him there was a little flat hat and in the hat there were three coins.

When we stood at the ticket machine he raised a hand vaguely in my direction.

He said, "Change—change."

I said, "I haven't got anything. Sorry."

He sagged back against the wall into the heap of his shawl and his face tipped into shadow.

We bought two tickets from the machine in the direction of the suburbs.

There was barely anyone on the train when it came: a

man with a little girl sitting down at the far end and a woman alone. The man and the little girl were reading a storybook. He read it out loud and every so often the child interrupted him in a small high voice.

The woman sat on her own on the other side of the carriage and watched them.

The light in the compartment was white and harsh and now and again one of the long lighting tubes would flicker for a moment. The floor was gray plastic and in the corners of the carriage the plastic was peeling back and there was metal underneath.

Cal and I sat in one corner beside the window.

I didn't feel like talking. Once he put his hand beside mine on the seat and our hands touched together and I wasn't sure whether it was an accident or deliberate but I moved my arm away.

Outside the window the city moved past: underbellies of viaducts with their great fat concrete legs in mud and sprawling weeds, pools of flat stagnant water with heavy rafts of green slime. Large areas of La Maya had to be held up out of the swampy ground. Walls were covered with graffiti: random obscenities; twisted faces; eyes, double rows of painted eyes, staring down.

– – –

Here and there, furtive wet movements in the dark which were maybe alligators.

And a few lines of a song turning round and round in my head: *a friend of the Devil is a friend of mine, if I get out before daylight . . .*

And there was the reflection of my face in the window-pane and it was faint and marooned against the colder pale of the carriage behind me.

7

A little mess of streets made up the outskirts of La Maya. We arrived close to midnight at the train station and walked down bungalow rows looking for the house number. The air was loud with cicadas and fainter drifting sirens, and yellow streetlights made the small equal front lawns yellow, and the doors too, and the shining gold numbers on the doorposts were the only things that varied from house to house.

Cal's friend lived in one of the bungalows at the end of a cul-de-sac. On the front lawn a plastic donkey was lying on its side amid grass tufts and an old car was parked up on blocks and overgrown with weeds.

The man who opened the door was small with short dark hair and a blunt squarish face and symmetrical features which were somehow pugnacious. His eyes were very dark.

His name was Maro.

He laughed and hugged Cal and said, "Come on in."

He poured glasses of whiskey for us in the big kitchen which must have taken up most of the ground floor. It was separated from the living area by bland islands topped with brown granite surfaces, ugly and highly polished and built around a black and silver oven. The living area was a half square of leather sofas that looked like they were made of plastic.

The sofas faced a television screen. Some comedy was playing with the volume turned down low so that all you could hear was the occasional muffled fug of laughter and it sounded like interference.

Maro had a big dog with a weighty head. Its slabs of jowls had drool hanging from them and its fur was stippled brown and black. When we first came into the front room the dog ran out from a hairy dog bed in the corner baying loudly and was held back by Maro who said, "She's fine, she's sweet," until eventually she subsided back into the corner and locked eyes with Cal. From there she let out the occasional quiet rippling growl. I could see him trying not to look at her.

Cal took Maro to one side in the kitchen and they spoke quietly.

I couldn't hear what they were saying and I didn't care. The sofa was deep and soft. My bones felt heavy and they dragged me down into it and there was a high buzzing whine in my ears. I felt a little punch-drunk, and there was something in the softness of the sofa that made me want to cry with relief and I didn't want that to happen.

The whiskey was sweet and acrid and I didn't like it. It sat hot in the back of my throat.

Maro said, "You all right there?"

"Yeah. Good. Thanks."

"Look about wiped out."

I fabricated a smile.

"You ever been down this way before?"

"Never."

"Oh? What do you think of it?"

I thought that he was trying to put me at my ease, and I disliked being talked to for the sake of talking. I wondered how much Cal had told him about why we were here. Probably he just thought I was some girl a long way from home and caught up in the charisma of Cal, a girl who Cal had made an effort to catch up because she was pretty, but who was tonight just tired and anxious and homesick. He must have seen a few girls like that because Cal must have had a few.

I shrugged and said, "It's different."

"I guess it would be."

Cal said, "Where's Kelsey?"

Maro swirled his drink. He said, "Kelsey took off."

"Sorry, man. When?"

"Four days ago. She's with her sister right now. Crazy bitch."

"Kelsey?"

"The sister. Crazy. Slagging me off all the time." He shrugged, gave an attempt at a laugh. It sounded flat. "Anyway. I give her a few days. She'll come around."

"Sorry, man."

"Yeah."

Maro said, "I've got some friends coming over later. It was already arranged and I didn't know you guys would be here. Hope you don't mind."

Cal said, "Of course not. Appreciate you having us."

From its limp cushion across the room the dog stared at us, growling.

When the friends arrived there were three men and two women and I could see Cal looking at the women. One of them was very pretty. She had dark hair and I noticed that she also looked often at Cal and probably if I hadn't been there they would have slept together or something like that.

They were all loud and Maro and Cal became loud to match them.

We sat out in the backyard on plastic chairs and everything was half-lit from the TV which was still on inside the room. Some of Maro's friends knew Cal already, not through Maro, just by chance. They had met up north and Cal had actually worked with one of them for a while.

The girl with dark hair said, "Crazy how people come around. Small world."

Cal made jokes and said clever things and they all laughed at his jokes.

He became very funny when he was drunk.

He moved rapidly between subjects, constantly talking but never becoming boring or flat or uninteresting. That was because he didn't say things with the intention of filling silence or even to have anybody listen, although everybody did listen to him because he was sharp and magnetic and also sometimes odd which was appealing, and he was always rolling a joint between his fingers or doing something with his hands.

Cal liked to make people laugh and for them to think he was funny, he liked showing people he was clever.

With a captive audience he became more expansive and sometimes a little arrogant and this arrogance was innate in him and he reveled in it and didn't try to hide it.

In the beginning I had found it very captivating.

The smoke had made my brain slow down. I felt it slowing. My head and my voice were full of fug and the sounds of the people speaking were swimming to me from a little distance away through a thick darkness.

Later after everyone else had left, Cal and I sat close together on the lawn chairs, and there was the smell of him which was smoke and aftershave and masked sweat.

I tried not to notice it.

At times, after he was gone, I had thought in passing moments in some bar or train station that I had caught a whiff of his smell and it had been the thing that could still drag out my guts, long after I had become used to the idea of his leaving. I could see photos and old possessions and whatever and stay even and numb and blank, but then one half-certain catch of it and that pain would come back and it felt like people were walking with heavy shoes on those spread guts.

It was thick with memories and so I tried to ignore it.

The slow feeling was in my arms and my legs and my brain and there was the outline of his face very near to mine in the dark. His features were blurred and softened and more like the old ragged Cal I remembered, not this new Cal which was him but hidden, him but warped, muted and buried under constructs of something else.

I looked away.

He said, "Maro can help us get a car. He has his old one in the front and he'll give it to us cheap."

I raised my eyebrows. "Us?"

He shrugged. "I thought we should stay together for a little while. Until we know what we're going to do."

I paused. After a moment I said, "OK. That sounds OK."

"Yeah?"

"How will we pay for it?"

He pulled at the cigarette and held in the smoke for a long moment and then exhaled. He said, "It's on credit for now. Maro's a good friend. He knows I'll get his money to him as soon as I have something together."

"Cal?"

"Anne Marie."

"What were you doing? Up north."

"Repairing cars."

"You weren't just repairing cars. You owed."

His face was in profile, sweep of bone with a cigarette at the end.

He said, "You won't like it, it was nothing smart. I got into some trouble, and I borrowed money. Some friend of some guy who worked with me at the garage. I knew what it was but I didn't have much of a choice at the time. I made a bad mess of things, Anne Marie." He stared into the dark, and then after a moment shrugged brusquely and flicked ash off the cigarette and said, "Doesn't matter much now. I suppose we should start thinking about where we need to go."

"I suppose."

"Where do you want to go?"

"I don't know."

He shrugged. "Then we'll figure it out. That's one for tomorrow."

There was silence.

Then I said, "Cal."

"Yeah."

"How are you so OK?"

He paused for a moment and then lit the new cigarette he had been rolling and blew a long stream of smoke. It hung in the light from the house windows.

After a moment he said, "I don't know. I wasn't at first."

Cicadas whirred off in the dark of the catalpa trees.

He said, "Are you doing all right? If you need—"

"I don't really want to talk about it. Not yet."

He nodded and looked down at the ground and traced his foot along the lines of the paving stones.

I saw the movements out of the corner of my eye without fully looking at him.

He said, "I should have been there for you. These past few years."

We were both silent for a moment.

Then I said, "I learned to be alone," because there was no way to say what I really needed to say and I wondered if he could understand that.

He said, "I know."

Then he said, "I'm sorry I left you, Anne Marie."

I stared down at the ground and my eyes were suddenly stinging and to make them stop I began some banality and he held up a hand before I could and said, "No—you don't need to get like that, because I'm not trying anything. This isn't me trying anything. But I wanted to say I'm sorry. Really. That was wrong. I shouldn't have done it."

In the long late nights alone in the kitchen of my apartment or the long late nights alone in a dark bedroom beside some blank attractive body that I didn't care about, I had gone over and over in my head what I needed to say to him, and I found that now that the chance was here to pull it out of myself and throw it ugly and heaving at his feet I had lost the capability to do it.

I said, "It was a long time ago."

A moment passed and then I turned and looked at him and asked, "Did you ever love me? Honestly."

"Honestly?"

"Yeah."

"I don't know. I don't think so. No."

I nodded. "That's what I thought. I wanted to be sure."

There had been something strained in his voice and it seemed that I saw all of him for a moment very clearly and I knew what was going to happen and felt blank and not at all the way I had thought I would feel and he kissed me and I kissed him back and there was the dry taste of cigarettes and the sour taste of alcohol.

He smelled warm.

I closed my eyes and felt sick at myself and didn't care and there was a blind rushing in my head, and there was Cal and the touch of his hand in my hair and there was his smell of sweat and dust and cigarettes which were metal and earth, and it was something, at least, it was something, it was changed and it was not intimacy but it was closeness and for a while I was not alone.

It was something.

I let my mind swell up and fill me with a roar in my ears and my brain.

8

- - - - - - -

Maro had left us the spare bedroom of the house.

It was small and against one wall there was a shoe rack full of women's shoes and on the wall there was a big framed photo of a woman standing beside a brown horse. The woman had black hair. She was laughing and her teeth were very white.

I could see her white teeth in the picture even in the near darkness of the room.

Cal and I were on top of the covers among fluffy pink pillows in the shape of hearts and afterward he turned away from me and fell asleep almost right away without saying anything and I lay awake in the dark.

There were photos tacked up everywhere on the walls, little Polaroid prints, and they were of groups of smiling friends and horse rides and nights out and they were all annotated in luminous white marker: *the girls at Luxe, Jo's Bachelorette, love u Ma, all my besties.*

One of her and Maro in a silver frame beside the bed.

On the bedside table the green numbers on the little alarm clock changed.

Cal was snoring slightly. An ugly sound at the back of his throat.

I don't know why and it was probably because my brain was exhausted and strained and caught in an overtired delirium on the edge of real sleep but his snoring made me think about the two wet heavy bags which were his lungs hemmed in by meat and full of the intricacies of alveoli, which were the tiny bags through which gases changed places within the big bag of the lung.

I had to sleep.

Cal's body was burning with heat in the little room and there was sweat on his skin and sweat on my skin and I rolled over and couldn't cool down. After a moment I turned onto my side and put the palm of my hand against the flat of his wrist on the pillow and tried to find familiarity there and couldn't.

The next morning Cal and I dressed in silence.

I avoided his eyes.

As I was walking past him to leave the bedroom he caught hold of my hand and tried to draw me toward him and I pulled away and he stepped back and there was something like surprise or confusion in his face and then he gave a wry half smile and pushed brusquely past me into the corridor.

Dimly after a few moments I heard the sound of him talking in the kitchen.

I waited alone in the bedroom for a while and the girl in the photograph on the wall stared at me with her white smile.

I came into the kitchen and Maro gave me coffee and Cal got up from the table quickly as soon as I entered the room and began washing the dishes at the sink with his back turned to me.

Cal never washed the dishes.

Maro looked at him for a long moment with his eyebrows raised and he was smirking a little.

He said to me, "Help yourself to breakfast. There's toast, there's cereal."

"Thanks."

"When you've eaten come out in the yard to take a look at this car. See what you two think."

The car that was parked on the edge of the lawn was painted red which had faded and there was rust on it. One of the doors had been replaced and was a different color and also had rust on it.

Cal said, "Will it go?"

And Maro hesitated and then said, "Yeah. Sure," dubiously, and we all stared at the car in silence.

Then Maro said, "I need it off the lawn, man. I'd be scrapping it otherwise."

I shrugged. I said, "It's fine. If it drives, it's fine."

Cal snorted and opened the driver's door and got in. The seat was set very close to the steering wheel and it was too close for his legs so that his legs were folded sharply up.

He pulled at the lever and tried to move it backward and nothing happened. He pushed against the seat hard with his back. Nothing happened.

Maro said, "Yeah. Sorry, man. That's jammed."

"Shit."

"Sorry."

"I'm supposed to drive with my knees under my chin?"

Maro shrugged. "You don't have to take it."

"We want the car."

We took out the backseats to free up space and left them on the front lawn and the dog slumped down and began to chew at them.

As we drove away from Maro's place he stood in the

middle of the driveway with one hand up in the air and standing there he made a small boxy figure.

For some reason as we left I found myself wondering if Maro's girl would ever come back to him. I felt that I would never go down his way again to find out and so I'd probably never know.

I don't know why that struck me the way it did and I don't know why that seemed so important, of everything that had happened in the past few days.

There was just something about it that I couldn't get out of my head.

The Polaroid photos on the wall and the white writing and the row of shoes left by the door.

9

- - - - - - -

That night we slept beneath a tree in the corner of a supermarket parking lot on the edge of La Maya. The concrete
of the parking lot was flat and washed out in the glare of
pale lights which stayed on all night and the supermarket
windows spilled light too.

Once I went in to use the bathroom at about two in the
morning and I opened the door of the car slowly so the
noise wouldn't wake Cal.

Inside the supermarket, workers looked drowned and
their eyes were faintly ringed with blue.

My reflection in the bathroom mirror was like that too.
My face looked thin and so did my wrists. My skin looked
gray. There was nobody else there and I stared at my reflection for a long time, at the gray print of myself, and

somehow I was very aware of my skin stretching over the bones of my face and I could almost feel it, that tension, and I could feel, too, the separation of me, of my bony gray body alone on a reflected field of white tiles and I felt the space around me with no one else there to break it. I seemed so odd, a small odd construction of white bone and slick red muscle and nameless yellow sludge all tied up with sinews and tendons and packaged mechanically to stand or fall.

I closed my eyes and there were bad pictures in my head, a prone shape on an alley floor and my hands held in Cal's, seeping red in a sink full of blood and water, and so I opened them again.

When I went back to the car the heat that had built up inside hit me when I opened the door. Cal lay on top of a blanket with his arms outstretched and his legs cramped, his torso twisted, and I hesitated for a moment and then curled up beside him with my hands around my chest and my skin sticky with heat, and in his sleep he moved toward me.

That night I thought about my mother.

Her name was Sarah van Rijk.

She had liked old films and classical guitar and we had listened to old music together.

She'd worked in a small office and she had been with three other girls in that office and they had made fun of her for liking classical guitar and playing it on the radio on her lunch breaks. She couldn't play herself but I know she always wanted to.

She bought a guitar once.

She saved up a long time for it and then she bought it and it had a shoulder strap with red and pink and orange and yellow triangles.

She bought some books to help her learn to play and the books had instructions in them and pictures of hands making different shapes on the neck of a guitar.

I used to hear her trying to practice in the front room of the little bungalow house late at night after I had gone to bed.

She never really managed to learn and one day she put the guitar up in the attic and I asked her why she had put it up there and she said she didn't have time to play it ever.

I think she was ashamed.

She was ashamed that she could never manage to play the music she loved so much.

Where's your mother? somebody said to me once. And I lied and said she had moved away and lived with her new husband. I was fifteen. I was living with my aunt and uncle, who were Tricia's mother and father. I had moved in with them.

My mother had just died.

They had a house on the north side of town, an ugly house, and there was a small lawn outside, just a few square feet, and my aunt had strange laws about people walking on that lawn. All of it was run around and held in by this little box hedge and then on the other side of the box hedge was the street and my uncle's parked car and then a few blocks away from that there was the sea which was not loud like the sea in San Padua, and so all you could hear in that house at night was the road outside, the sound of shouting kids in the evening, and then later the rush of passing cars.

It was colder up there.

Anyway.

Someone asked me where my mother was and I told them she had gone away. I said *she's gone away with her new husband.*

And they said *why didn't you go with her* and I shrugged and said I didn't want to, *she moves too much.*

I still don't know why I lied about that.

10

- - - - - - -

The next morning I took my first stint of driving.

I drove south, mainly on impulse.

It was a hot day and there was sweat under my armpits and in the crook of my elbows and all around the seams of my shorts which were digging into my thighs and making them sore. I kept shifting positions. We stopped for a bathroom break at a gas station and there was a red line on the top of each of my legs.

Cal went into the bathroom and I waited outside. To my right there was a doughnut and coffee place with orange plastic tables and there was a sticker on the window which made up one wall and in the corner there were tall wheeled racks with slats to put your used trays into, and the trays were covered with red paper cups and plastic straws and paper napkins and odds and ends of food packaging.

There was a long line of people at the doughnut counter. They were slack-faced with the early morning.

Two little kids ran about between the tables and after a moment one of them fell and began to cry and the mother came over and picked it up and said something which was maybe comforting or maybe admonishing.

Beside me was a newsstand with newspapers and magazines and I wandered over to look at it. Toward the bottom of the front page of the newspaper, underneath the headlines, were the words:

BODY FOUND IN SAN PADUA KILLING

The body of a man was discovered in the early hours of Tuesday morning in Tana Beach, a notorious neighborhood of San Padua. The area, well known for its nightclubs, bars and brothels, has seen a spike in violent crime over the past year. The victim was identified as Sandro Martin, a man in his late twenties. The police have so far declined to comment. An investigation is ongoing.

Cal came up behind me and stopped.

I murmured, "Cal."

He said, "Yeah. I know. Come on. Don't read it."

He moved me away toward the doors.

Before he did I saw the photo below the article and it was the face of Sandro Martin, the man in the alley.

He had dark hair and his face was pale.

His eyes were dark blots of ink and they bored into me.

In the car Cal said, "Don't think about it. You can't go there."

I stared ahead of me.

Those two dark eyes, those two blots of ink.

In front of the gas station a woman was dragging a child by the hand and I watched them without really seeing them.

After a moment I said, "I can't not think about that, Cal."

Then I said, "The police are looking."

"Let them look."

"How can you say that?"

He said, "We'll face bad things when they happen. If they happen. They won't."

"You can't just assume."

"They won't."

That was the first time I had really seen the man's face. I thought, Jesus Christ, I didn't even know what he looked like.

Jesus.

He had been an ugly man. An ugly heavy man and his face could have been any other heavy face.

I tried to get them out of my head, those two dark eyes which were two lumped clumps of ink from a printing press, all pixelated, and I couldn't, and they were there and they bored into my mind's eye, and that heavy ugly face warped and became a strange botched version of itself in my memory.

Back on the road we rolled both windows down in the front of the car but I could still smell sweat, my own sweat and his, the warm tang of it, it was on my clothes and my hair.

I thought, I need a shower.

I felt dirty. I felt filthy, running deeper than skin.

Early that morning I had tried to clean off the animal smell at a roadside service station where there had been a sort of foot wash, I think it was, and it was outside at the corner of the building and I had crouched down and stuck my head under it and then my arms and legs. There had been a car hovering about behind me. It was waiting to go to the car wash. There was a family inside it and they had watched me, dull, incurious, faces sagging.

I felt my own filth sitting on me.

On the dashboard there was an empty orange juice

bottle and a paper coffee mug and a folded chicken sandwich wrapper that was spotted a little with mayonnaise and all these things were heating in the sun and the smell was making my head ache.

I wondered if people had smelled this way before we wore clothes. Surely they hadn't with bodies open to the air and bodies open to rainwater with nothing to trap all your own dirt to you.

"I feel unclean," I said.

He snorted. "Better get used to it. Anyway. We are unclean."

"I smell."

"I like your smell."

Despite myself I laughed a little. "No you don't. Not like this."

"I love your dirt."

I said, "Don't."

"What?"

"You know what."

After a moment he said, "I like what you really are."

I looked sharply over to him and tried to read his face, to see whether he was just saying what he thought I wanted to hear, and it was impossible to tell because he always looked like he meant what he was saying. He caught my eyes and smiled.

I don't know if there's anyone in the world who can say *I like what you really are* to another person and mean it.

We stopped at a gas station. On the roof was a giant plastic chicken and coming out of its mouth was a giant plastic speech bubble. Inside the speech bubble were the words:

SEE YOU NEXT TIME, FOLKS

Behind the building there was a small lawn with a couple of picnic tables on dead grass.

I climbed up and sat on top of one and Cal sat beside me and took a pack of cigarettes from his pocket and took one out and lit it and put it in his mouth and then lit another and passed it to me.

I said, "Thanks."

I looked across at him. He was leaning back, slouching back, and his face was tipped up slightly to the sky. And his shirt was stained and hanging open and the sleeves were rolled up and I could see the tops of his arms where they were a little burned and starting to peel. And I could smell him and he smelled of cigarettes and joints and bad aftershave and chewing gum and old breath and fried takeout food.

He looked sideways at me and our eyes caught and he smiled a half-twist smile and I looked away but I was smiling too despite myself.

He nodded up at the back of the plastic chicken and he said, "It's someone somewhere's job to make those."

"Someone somewhere."

"Poor bastard."

He was quiet for a moment. Then he said, "Scares me out of my mind."

"What does?"

"That. Day in, day out, standing in some production line pressing a button or whatever. Like my father did."

"I know. I remember."

"Worked in a car factory every day of his life more or less, right up till he could barely walk through the door. Then they let him have a couple of years sitting in some chair in front of a TV screen. With his loving wife." For a moment he stared straight ahead and his eyes were sealed off, glazed. Then he spat on the ground and stubbed out the cigarette under his shoe and said, "Anyway. Long time since we had anything to do with each other, me and him." He turned to me. "You ready to go?"

"Yeah. Let's go."

Driving down onto the highway, I could see the shape of his body out of the corner of my eye, slumped against the car door in the passenger seat.

Just for a moment he looked somehow smaller and shrunk in on himself.

In front of me the long length of the road wound out, wound out and wound on under hot sky.

And I drove and the road became hypnosis, a horizon and an end point in perpetual retreat, one long reel of flashing gray and cat's-eyes.

And low in front of me the old wavering sun.

We turned off the main highway into swampy land with plane trees plate-like on a late yellowish sky and grasses and shining brown water broken by the snarls of great fallen branches all bleached out and covered in egrets, and occasionally the heads of alligators, snout and yellow eyes, and here and there were traces of people, some mining holes filled with water, a luminous chemical blue, and heavy heaps of mulch beside them, and the length of road empty in front of me cutting through and cutting on.

We drove through miles of swampland stretching bright with water in the late sun and we came to a new road as the sun went down somewhere to the right of us, flooding yellow onto the bottom of a deep blue sky, a few stars winking low on the horizon.

We were silent and tired.

I looked over at Cal.

His head was slumping forward on his chest. Every now and again there would be a movement as he jerked awake.

I put on the radio. There was some old song playing, blues, a male singer. His voice was sad.

It sat on the hot air.

It made me feel old.

I used to have dreams when I was very young of being a huge bodiless expanse of consciousness without end and I would wake up scared and wanting to go back into my body and at the same time exhilarated. It was something like vertigo, and every so often as an adult I've had vague hints, intimations of the same feeling, a sort of brush of a memory of it at the edge of my mind. I try to hold on to it and magnify it, but I can never quite get at it or draw it out enough to fill me up.

But I feel myself at the edges of it sometimes.

That night driving on that highway with the blotched sunset on deep dark and the few faint stars, I felt it then, the memory of vertigo.

11

- - - - - - -

We swapped seats.

Cal told me to sleep. It was getting late, almost eleven. He wanted to wind a path back to the coast to find somewhere to park for the night. I closed my eyes with my head half on the plastic of the doorframe and half on the cold glass of the window above it and vibrations against my cheek and the seat belt cutting into my neck.

I was exhausted but I didn't want to sleep. My brain was wired and my thoughts were hectic and a little delirious and anxious and buzzing round and round in my head.

So I pretended to be asleep and through my half-closed eyes I watched the vague rhythmic flicker of headlights going past and I listened to the faint crumple of static laughter on the radio.

Then I must really have fallen asleep because I was walking alone in a deserted airport which meant I was dreaming. I was in a long white terminal building and there were rows and rows of airport chairs stretching out a long way ahead of me and there were big signs hanging down from the ceiling. When I tried to read them I found that the names were not real at all but instead were random letters scrambled up with no order.

All the other people at the airport must already have left to get on their flights because there was only me still there alone and staring up at these signs, trying to decode them, and it seemed like the more I looked the more the letters danced and moved and slipped away.

And suddenly I found myself not alone anymore but arguing with a shop attendant who had appeared out of nowhere in the little airport news kiosk.

I was trying to buy a newspaper and the woman had hold of one end of it and I had hold of the other and she was pulling it out of my hands.

"It's not in the right language, it's all backward," she was saying. "You can't read it anyway."

"But I need it."

"You can't. You're not supposed to. We're closed."

"But I have to see—"

I tugged it hard and it came out of her hands and on the front page was the photo that I had known would be there, the spread-eagled body, the running blood pixelated into the gutter of the road and all of it splashed out in blurred ink and strangely distorted, Sandro Martin flooding the inside of his head onto the tarmac.

I woke to the feeling of the plastic door handle digging into my back; Cal was shaking my shoulder.

It was pitch dark.

He said, "Are you all right?"

"Fine."

"Are you sure? You were talking in your sleep."

"I'm fine." There was heaviness in my eyes and it was thick and dark. "Where are we?" My voice was dry.

"At the coast. Near a place I used to come on vacation with my family when I was a kid."

Outside there was the sound of water, soft wavelets.

I opened the door.

Low old trees grew together overhead and their branches were bleached white and twined and smooth and hung with thick pads of draping moss and their flat glossy leaves were murmuring in the night breeze.

We were parked in a sandy clearing and there were trees surrounding us and the road was winding back behind. In front of us there was an opening in the trees and through it was the flat darkness of the ocean.

Tiny waves broke on the sand, white on black.

I climbed out of the passenger seat and walked across the clear space and into the water barefoot and there were stars above me and the smell of salt in my throat and I looked up at the sky and raised my hands above my head and turned around and around in the water under the huge clarity of the dark sky and the stars which stabbed out long points of light.

Cal walked out and stood beside me and his face was turned upward.

After a moment he made a half movement in the water and put his arms around my shoulders and for a moment we leaned, slumped against each other, exhausted, and I felt myself swaying and I thought I would fall but didn't. I closed my eyes and there was stillness and the ragged sound of my own breath and the warmth of his body pressed against my back. I said, "I have to sit down."

I pulled away from him and walked out and sat down on the sand of the beach and looked out at the water and Cal came and sat beside me.

I said, "I've been thinking about where we should go. I thought maybe we should go to Eidon."

"Eidon? That's farther south. What would we do there?"

I shrugged. "I don't know. Whatever we'd do anywhere else, I suppose. I want to see the mountain, Eidon Mountain. Have you seen it?"

"Yeah. There's snow on the peak in the middle of summer. The city is built out across the valley."

"I want to see it."

He shrugged in the dark. "We can go there. If it's what you want."

Then he said, "And what about when we get there?"

"What do you mean?"

He paused. He was staring at the water and his face was fixed and he seemed to be looking through it and not really seeing it.

Then he said abruptly, "What was the other night to you? At Maro's."

"Where did that come from?"

"I don't know."

"It's not like you. To talk."

He shrugged. "I just wondered."

I paused for a moment and foundered but he didn't seem to need an answer. I thought maybe he hadn't expected one.

After a while he said, "You know, you were always

above the rest for me, Anne Marie. You were always above the others."

"Cal—"

"Just let me say it. I know I wasn't right to you and I know I broke things. But I did want to make it work."

I looked at his face in the moonlight and it cut me to my gut. I said, "You could've told me you were leaving. I'd have let you go because I would've done anything for you, Cal. Anything to see you happy, even if it meant giving you up."

"I know, shit, I know—"

"That's what broke me. That you didn't tell me, and that I never really knew what was in your head."

He was silent for a moment and then when he spoke his voice was hoarse. He said, "I have this feeling, this smothering feeling, and it's pressing on me all the time and it's like I'm burning up against the whole world and the only way to escape it is to move, to keep moving so it doesn't catch up with me. Sometimes it goes away when I drink, when I come close to some kind of an edge. But it always comes back. I remember being in that apartment we had and thinking it's got me again, it's got me here too, the feeling's back. I tried to ignore it. I tried not to give in."

"But you did. And this is where we are." For a moment I felt so tired and far away from him.

Silence fell and we sat side by side, looking out over the dark.

Eventually he said, "Yeah. This is where we are."

Somewhere out across the water a bird keened in the night, and its sound went on and on through the stillness.

12

Here is a memory about Cal.

We met at a party near Tana Beach and it was in a sweat-filled nightclub that spewed out noise and splayed stumbling people down a little side alley set back from the sea. The walls of that alley were plastered over with posters for music festivals and parties that were out of date and the colors were fading away and their edges were peeling off and flapping in the hot night breeze.

And there was a metal door at that nightclub, I remember the metal door, on rollers that opened and closed. It was covered in graffiti and flyers like the walls of the alley and there was an ugly old bouncer who stood leaning to one side.

Anyway.

I was there with a few friends. Back then I was living in the first apartment I had ever had on my own, not an apartment really, but a living room with a sofa bed in the corner. There was an actual bedroom in that place too and the bedroom was owned by my roommate whose name was Mimi, as she had been in the apartment first. I didn't mind, or at least I don't remember minding.

I had not known Mimi before I moved in. She'd written a For Rent notice on a small piece of paper and pinned it to a bulletin board in a supermarket and my aunt, who I had been living with before, had found it and written down the number and given the number to me. At the time my aunt and I were not getting along well. I was in my final year of school and I wanted to leave.

The place was small and dingy and the white walls were so old they were turning gray. There was a little sort of kitchenette in one corner of the living room on the opposite side from my bed, so that one corner was the kitchen and one corner was the bedroom and then everything in between was the living room, and all my life at the time was held between the pale grayness of those walls, boxed in there.

Right after I went to live with Tricia, I moved to her school on the other side of town because my aunt and uncle thought it would be easier for us to go to the same place, and they thought it would be better for me.

They said *this will be better for you.*

Tricia was a few years ahead of me in school, and I didn't know anybody. She tried to look out for me and in the beginning she would come looking for me at break times and in between classes and say *are you all right* and I would say *yes.* But the school was big and she was busy and went to sports clubs and had friends and as the months went by she came to look for me less and less.

Other kids at school didn't like me.

There was this one girl called Anita who once tried to push me over a double row of desks for no reason, and I turned around and lashed out and caught her full in the face. I think it surprised her.

It surprised me.

And I felt at first shocked and then loose and euphoric and not guilty until much later.

I found that the teachers didn't like to say anything to me because of my mother.

Instead they would take me to one side and tell me they wanted a word.

"Are you happy with yourself, Anne Marie?"

"I don't know, sir."

"Are you proud of yourself?"

"I don't know."

"Don't you want to be proud of yourself?"

"I don't know. Should I?"

At first they all looked at me the same way, which was a little pitying and also a little irritated, and then after a while I think their patience wore thin and they weren't pitying anymore.

They moved me down a few sets and for the most part let me slip off into the unseen.

By then I was fighting with my aunt and she found the number for this place and I moved out and the girl Mimi was nice enough. I was working in this pizza place a few streets away and that was nice enough too and I could have free pizza and survive off the scrounged crusts left greasy in their cardboard boxes on the street tables outside, and I always smelled of takeout and of frying things.

Then I met Cal.

I had gone out with a group of Mimi's friends, not mine, but they were good enough people and they had come around to the apartment first of all because it was the birthday of one or other of them, and then they had said *let's go to Blue Lagoon*, which was the name of the club where the party was, and so we had gone to Blue Lagoon, the sleazy alleyway place with the metal door.

The music was bad and yammering and the people were too close.

I turned around and there was someone behind me and it was Cal although I didn't know that then. I looked at this person between a few moving bodies, and there was an odd frozen moment which sounds stupid and false but that's how it felt, and I was caught there suddenly in the way he was looking at me, the intensity, and the moment stretched and stretched and then went by.

He pushed through a few other people and came over and asked me my name.

I found out later he was supposed to be there on a date, but I never saw her and he never left my side.

Later we walked out together.

It was a hot night and the heat held down on us, and there was the sound of the waves and over that almost as loud the drilling of the cicadas in the palm trees on the avenue at the end of the alley, the avenue that led to the sea, and when we got down onto the sand there was the paleness of the beach in the dark and away to one side the ocean flat and black and showing as a rip in the bottom of the sky. To our other side the lights of the crumbling city lined red and orange and yellow along the oceanfront and stretched away in a muddled chain, and Cal and I stood on the sand in the middle of everything.

The two of us were small under the vault of the universe.

13

- - - - - - -

Tricia called me one evening.

Cal was driving and it was late and the sun was setting over the swamp to our left, slow and red, spools of green hanging in the old trees standing white and bleached in the water, branches full of egrets, wide rafted thickets of vegetation and water-lily leaves and bubbled hulks of algae.

I had forgotten to contact her. We hadn't spoken in the five days or so since I had left San Padua and the moment she called I felt a bolt of anxiety in my stomach.

"Anne Marie, where are you?" The line was bad. Her voice sounded very far away.

I said, "I can't hear you very well."

"I said, where are you? One of those girls you share the

apartment with got in touch. Apparently I'm your secondary contact number. She found it through the landlord."

I said, "I'm not in San Padua."

"What? Why?"

"I left."

"I can't hear you."

"I *left*."

"You mean you're not there?"

"No."

"What? Are you going back?"

"I don't know."

"My God, Anne Marie. Where are you? Who are you staying with? Are you safe? What's going on?"

"It's OK. It's OK. I'm south of La Maya. I'm with Cal."

A moment of crackling silence on the line. Then she said, "You've lost your mind."

"Tricia—"

"You have honestly lost your mind."

"It's not what you think."

"Don't go back there, Anne Marie. Please. Not for me, for yourself."

There was shouting in the background at her end of the line.

She said, "Christ, these kids."

I said, "I'm OK, Tricia. Don't worry about me, OK?"

"Will you tell me where you're going?"

"South. Eidon City."

"You're going there? Why on earth are you going there?"

"I don't know."

"What do you think you're planning to do?"

"Find a job, I suppose. Find an apartment."

"Anne Marie, at least say you'll let me know if you're not safe. If you're in trouble. I want to know you're looking after yourself."

"Of course I'm looking after myself."

"You know I'm two hours away from Eidon. If anything goes wrong, if you need anything, you call me, all right? I have a car. I'll come and get you, Anne Marie."

"Thanks, Tricia."

There was a pause.

After a moment she said, "Don't go too far away."

I had a sort of vague intimation of what she meant and it scared me because I could feel how easy it would be to do it.

After I put the phone down Cal said, "That was about me, wasn't it?"

I paused.

I said, "Yeah. Sort of. Some of it." He was silent.

I looked over at him and saw that he was smiling.

"Were you in love before me?"

I said, "Yes."

Cal said, "You never told me that before. I always sort of assumed you weren't. Is that strange?"

I shrugged.

He said, "You were so young. I just thought you wouldn't have been."

We stopped in a little diner by the side of the road. It was night. We had driven all day.

It was raining heavily outside and it had been since the early morning, the smell of wet heat rolling in from the land. Now the rain made starbursts on the window beside our table. I could hear it tinny on the metal roof. It drowned out the sound of the TV playing in the far corner of the restaurant, playing on the music channel, muscular girls with shiny bodies writhing onscreen. They kept perfect formation, became small moving points.

He said, "What happened there?"

I said, "We loved each other but we were too different. It was the wrong time in our lives. We wanted different things."

That was a lie, an inanity. That wasn't what had happened.

I told Cal that lie because it was something of mine I wouldn't show to him. A part of me that I kept from him, which was hurt and weak and small and petty and desperate and hungry. A part of me I had tried to show him once a long time ago. I used to think he could see it.

The man I had been in love with before was called Matthew. I was seventeen and he was twenty-one and we'd met in the summertime, just as I was moving out of my aunt and uncle's and into Mimi's apartment. He was part of an extended group of friends, people I had spent my late teen years with, and he was a friend of a friend, some distant connection, and we had met one day at a party on the beach, and after a little while the police had shown up and told everyone to go home and stop being loud, and me and him had ended up wandering through the city in the dark watching the long hoop shadows of street cats on house walls. After that we had begun to see each other. He used to pick me up after my shift at the bakery where I was working weekends and we would walk down onto the beach together. After about two months very much out of the blue he had told me he loved me and I hadn't said it back to him. I hadn't not said it because it wasn't true; I had been shocked by hearing it and I had been shy and afraid that I hadn't heard him properly. A man had never said that to me before.

So I hadn't said anything when he said it; I had only smiled at him, probably quite a useless limp smile looking back, which he must have taken to mean *no I don't feel the same way*, and so he hadn't said it again after that.

A week later he found out he'd got a job far across the country and it was a surprise because he hadn't expected to get that job and so he would be moving away and he didn't think whatever we were doing should continue, and I said *it's fine I'm not attached and there are no emotions I always knew it was just for the summer* and I lied to him because that wasn't true and I was in love with him and I was hurt that he was going but that wasn't what I told him. I said *I think I'll leave now* and didn't return his calls and then we didn't meet again until he had a going-away party with all our friends from home all together and there was some boy there and he was twenty or so, I think, a boy not a man, but he was good-looking enough and fun enough so I kissed him and was all over him like the young little girl that I was, and then I looked over and saw that Matthew was watching which was what I had wanted. But I realized in that moment that it wasn't what I wanted at all because I saw from his eyes that the angry things I had thought about him and the way that I had been hurt were wrong because he loved me, he really loved me, and I was not over there with him I was over here with this boy kissing my neck like a boy without control, and I went back home with that boy which was the first time I had gone home with someone I didn't know and that night I learned something about emptiness.

A few years later I met Cal and decided to align the course of my happiness with him and that was that.

But I wasn't ready to say that to Cal. I wasn't ready to

14

- - - - - -

Here is the story of my epiphany, brought to me by my husband Cal.

My Cal.

I thought he would stop me from being alone in my own head.

I pinned that expectation on another collection of cells who was just as lost and hopeless and confused at finding themselves in the unexpected state of being conscious as I was. And in there was my mistake, my huge steaming train wreck.

I used to believe that in life there was one man meant for one woman in a cosmic sense with me drawn to him and him to me by a great big movement of energy or the plan of the universe or the patterns of the stars.

I had high and secret ideals about love and I never told them to anyone so no one knew I had them.

Cal was my confirmation.

I used to believe that we, a little fringed-off species, isolated lumbering hunks of flesh, could truly know one another purely and selflessly.

Whatever that was supposed to mean.

I believed in love as an abstract concept, as an ideal, as the be-all and end-all goal that it was touted to be, as some kind of great curing resting place, the end point toward which the mass thoughts and life choices of a planet filled with tiny people sluggishly moved.

All that was really there was a game of evolution.

That was another cultural misstep in the wiring of my brain.

But I was very young when I met Cal.

It was a long time since I had swallowed shit like that.

15

- - - - - -

I was looking out of the window at the blur of the trees with my head leaning on the glass and my mind drifting, when beside me I heard Cal say "Shit, oh, shit," and I looked into the rearview mirror and there were blue lights flashing round and round and they were coming up fast around the other cars.

I said, "Get off the highway at the next right."

"No, wait. They might go past."

In the rearview the police car had slowed and begun to tail along behind us.

"Christ," I said. "They're following. They want us to pull over."

"I can see that, Anne Marie. I'm going to try to get off the highway."

"There's no exit. There's nowhere to get off."

The lights in the rearview went round and round.

Cal said, "Shit. I have to pull over."

"No, Cal, no—"

"I have to. Just don't panic. Act calm, OK? Act normal."

"I don't think I can—" I could feel panic rising up inside me.

"You can. You have to. Come on, Anne Marie."

A little way up ahead there was a rest area and Cal pulled into it and wound down the window.

After a moment the police car appeared alongside us.

In the driver's seat was a policeman and he wore a dark uniform and above the dashboard of his car hung a set of furry dice and I saw them swinging and felt a hysterical urge to laugh.

Cal leaned out of the window. He said, "Afternoon."

"Sir, I've been trying to get you to pull over for the last mile or two."

"Is there a problem?"

"I just wanted to tell you you've been going twenty above the speed limit since I started to follow you. Did you know?"

"I'm so sorry, Officer. My wife's sister is having a baby. We just had the call and we're trying to make it to the hospital."

"Is your wife's sister in the car?"

"No."

"Then don't let me catch you driving like that twice. If I see you doing that again on this road I'll slap a ticket on you."

"I appreciate the heads-up. It's the last time you'll see us. I promise."

"I hope so."

After he had gone we sat there in the rest area. I leaned my head against the back of the seat. I said, "I thought that was—"

"I know. So did I."

I heard him breathe out, a long breath, and it shook a little.

He said, "That was my fault. I was careless. Sorry. I won't do anything stupid like that again. I won't draw attention."

"Yeah."

"You all right?"

"Yeah."

He leaned over and put his hand on my shoulder and shook it gently and I stared ahead out of the window. "I won't do that again. I promise."

I nodded. "It's all right. Maybe I should drive for a while."

"OK."

I stared ahead out of the front windshield and waited for the sickness in my stomach to pass.

We wove down south through lush green that soon became the deep dry green of thorny forests. Miles and miles of trees and no houses and the one thin road going between them and lone buzzards wheeling above us and dead armadillos in the ditches and sometimes at night flashing white rumps of deer.

There was something unspoken between us.

We stopped to buy food at gas stations and fast-food places, which were few and far between here. For the first time we could drive for more than half an hour without seeing chain signs and when we stopped we both went in separately and walked around and bought something to eat and then we drove on without speaking.

Often Cal would pull in at the side of the road to smoke; a few times he lit up inside the front of the car when we were driving. I didn't like it but I didn't say anything.

Sometimes on those gas station food runs there would be a few police milling about in ones and twos in the foyers or buying cups of coffee from the tall machines and I would feel my palms begin to sweat and I would put my eyes to the ground and walk quickly past them.

Cal said to me once, "It's a good thing you're not a thief. You'd be found out pretty quick."

"I feel like they can see it. What we did. I feel like they can see through me, Cal."

"Well, they can't. Don't give them a reason to ask questions."

It came into my head at odd moments, the feel of it, the memory of sticky wetness on my skin, and the smell which was the slick opening of something.

It made my throat close.

When that happened I would fix my eyes on the trees outside the window and watch them go past very fast, the striations of the quick passing of their trunks, and breathe in and out until the feeling was gone.

I kept watching the newspaper headlines.

There had been two robberies in San Padua that month and one of them had been a bank on Farra Boulevard and the robbers had blown a big hole in the wall, and there had been three gang shootings and a wealthy tycoon was being blackmailed and the mayor had been caught with a prostitute and his wife had been evading taxes.

There was nothing more about Sandro Martin.

It became a fixation, reading those headlines. Sometimes I made up excuses to pull into service stations so I could read them in the news kiosks. I would say I needed the bathroom or I wanted a drink or something to eat and then I would go in there and look for those black blots of pixelated eyes that were Sandro Martin's eyes in that photograph, and they weren't there and I would get back in the car and Cal would look at me and I knew he knew what I was doing but he never said anything.

I don't know whether he was reading them too.

I didn't want to ask.

I began to crave driving at night. There was a different feel to it between the straight trees in blackness with just a few stars above the road and every now and again a lone truck, red and orange taillights and the reflection of my face in the car window, my reflection which was pale with dark eye wells. It used to give me a strange feeling to be on those roads in the dark; a strange sadness which was nothing to do with Cal, but some echo of those times before when I was a child with my mother, sitting in the backseat of the car while we were driving down a dark lane late at night under the cover of trees; a deep longing for something, and it was so strong it was almost a sickness and it was not quite a bad feeling but not quite a good one, nostalgia I suppose was the closest thing to it but it wasn't really nostalgia either, it was something more than that because it wasn't a desire to be back in the past and it wasn't a need for something I had and then lost, it was a need for something I had never had in the first place. And when I was driving down those dark roads I realized the person next to me was a stranger and also that most of the people I'd ever known were strangers, and I was sealed alone in the tight isolation chamber of my stupid thin-skinned head, my strange awkward skull, and suddenly I wanted this thing so badly and the sadness was there because I didn't know exactly what it was and I knew I would never be able to find it.

Once we parked up in the corner of a supermarket parking lot in the late evening.

Cal had been driving and he needed a break.

We sat in the car seats. In front of us a woman walked her little kid across the parking lot and she was pushing a stroller and the kid half ran along beside it and the kid had brown curly hair and wore a red shirt and he was chattering away to the mother and she was half listening, I thought, and half looking around her for oncoming cars.

From out of the stroller there rose a pink balloon on a string. It bobbed as the little group moved along.

The sight of the woman and her kids gave me a strange pang in my stomach.

16

- - - - - - -

One night we drove down a long forestry lane off the main highway to find somewhere to sleep.

We were about two days' drive from Eidon Mountain.

There was a little pebbled rest area in the woods for the logging trucks and it was edged with long wild grasses which gave way to the dark of the pine trees. We were ringed by them. Up above us was an oval of night sky full of stars and dark quick-moving clouds and wind moving the black treetops at its edge.

I got out of the car and walked to the edge of the trees and there was the smell of pine, sharp, and the wet smells of soil and moss on the breeze.

I had left my shoes in the footwell of the car and my feet were bare. Between tufts of grass there were pieces of gravel and they dug into the soles of my feet and the pain seemed to heighten the night and to sharpen it and it felt good.

Behind me I heard the driver door open and shut and then Cal's footsteps round the side of the car and the sounds of the side door opening; he was getting ready to sleep.

I breathed in the wet nighttime flavors of the air.

"Anne Marie?"

I turned. He had walked up behind me and was standing a little way away and he was looking at me. He seemed hesitant suddenly which was odd for him and I realized that he was unsure about whether he should come over to me and whether I would want him to come over to me. When I turned and walked toward him the moment was gone and the unsure look on his face was broken and something about that struck me deeply and I had the strangest feeling of walking toward him and studying him as I went, objectively for the first time in a long time, the first time since he had come back, the print of his face in the light from behind him through the open door of the car, how flat he suddenly seemed.

And I remembered another moment from a long time ago. The moment when I had seen that, for all of his wild carelessness, Cal too had a front like all the rest and it was just a different front and a different way to hide a frightened little brain full of lonely thoughts. I remembered the feeling that came with that because if Cal wasn't thinking what I was thinking then nobody was.

My mind was somewhere in the dark over the trees, disparate, around it an aching void of space.

Carefully he put his arms around me.

He said, "You're so different now, Anne Marie. You're different."

I laughed and I thought it sounded hollow maybe and I wondered if he could tell. I said, "What am I supposed to say to that?"

He stared at me for a moment and then shrugged. "Whatever you want. I don't know. You don't have to say anything."

"Cal, do you know—"

I stopped for a moment and looked at his face and felt for the right words and like always at times like this they weren't there.

I said, "Do you have any idea what I felt for you?"

"Jesus, Anne Marie. We're not going back there again—"

"No. No, you see? You're already backing straight back out."

"What? I'm not—"

"Cal. When we get to Eidon I don't know what's going to happen. I don't know where I'm going to go."

"What are you saying you want?"

"I don't know. I don't know yet."

He stared at me for a long moment and then he laughed and it was a little harsh.

He said, "This wasn't what I wanted to end up talking about at all."

I rubbed my eyes. "I know. Me neither, not now. I'm so tired, I need to get some sleep."

I watched him walk back to the car and I followed a little way behind and let him make up the blankets in the back into a sort of nest, and he crawled in before me through the side door and I went after him and lay in the sticky heat, in the closeness of the little car, the night cicadas loud outside, somewhere not so far away the sound of the highway which moved moved moved all night rushing on, and I wondered who was on that highway and what they were doing and what they were thinking and where they were going. And I thought that probably I would go my whole life without meeting a single one of those people moving in those cars and yet they had made this tiny little interaction, this tiny little piece that they had put into this night of my life, this piece that was each individual rushing sound of a moving car on a highway far away through a forest night.

And outside in the dark trees the cicadas droned on and on and got in my head and in my brain and lay over the moving of the blood in my ears until I couldn't tell the two sounds apart.

Cal fell asleep quickly.

He twitched slightly and ground his teeth together in his sleep.

I lay awake, and thought *where am I going,* and lay awake, and lay awake.

17

- - - - - -

What I am talking about now is something from a long time ago.

This is how he left me.

There was a distance in him for a while before that morning when I woke up and found that he was gone. I remember the feel of it and I could sense it and it made me desperate and afraid and it made me cling to him. I could feel that driving him further away and I had no way to stop myself and I hated myself for it and hated what I was doing and the way I was with him but I couldn't change. I held on tighter and tighter and I put my hands around his throat.

We could both feel something coming between us.

We skirted around it and it grew.

And then that one morning I woke up and there was a pale breeze in the room from the open window and he was gone.

And so then I did all those things that I thought would drown my mind and those things were the cold blank nights, the numb nights in unfamiliar houses staring at walls which were the walls of those men who I met in clubs and bars and who said *you're beautiful* or some such inanity and I gave them all the same blank smile and it said *take me home* and my mind behind it said *wake me up wake me up make me feel.*

And often I sat alone on the beach in the night with the faint sounds of the city behind me, and drank whiskey and looked up at spinning sprays of stars above the white of breaking surf in darkness and beyond that the black open flat of the ocean reaching out and out.

Then all of a sudden Cal came back and a man died in an alley in the dark.

18

- - - - - - -

The next day we broke down.

Cal was driving and we had just filled the car up with gas. We had gone together to pay for the fuel and to pay as well for a couple of bags of peanuts and potato chips and a loaf of bread and things like that. We had stood at the checkout in the gas station and at first Cal's card had been declined.

I stared at the card machine.

The woman said, "Let me just try that once more for you, sir."

I could see her half looking at us and I knew what she was thinking.

She scanned it again. It beeped.

She said, "That's accepted."

I felt Cal slacken a little with relief beside me.

Neither of us said anything about it afterward but it hung there unspoken.

And then after we had been driving along and playing blues on the radio and singing to it loudly a cloud of steam rose up from the hood and I said, "Cal, look at that," and he said, "No, it's fine, I worked as a mechanic up in Costa Maria, that's nothing to worry about," and then the car engine had gone put-put-put and Cal said, "Ah, shit," and we lost momentum and just cruised, just rolled while we gradually slowed down, until we finally stopped at the side of the road.

We both got out of the car.

The steam was thick and slightly black. There was a harsh smell.

Cal said, "Piece of shit."

I said, "I thought you were a mechanic in Costa Maria. Can't you fix it?"

"Don't be smart."

"I'm not."

We waved down a truck driver and he got out and came over and bent down, looking hard at the hood, which steamed darkly.

He said, "That's some heavy smoke you've got coming out of there."

"Yeah."

"How old is this thing? Looks like it's been running around since the sixties."

"Something like that."

"Well, man, there's not much I can do to help you. You need a mechanic. Maybe they can get it to limp a few more miles."

"Christ."

"Sorry."

"You think you could give us a ride to the nearest town?"

"Yeah, man. I'm only going that far. There's seats in front."

We walked over to the car and stood beside it while the driver went back to his cab.

Cal said to me, "Let's leave it here. Piece of junk, reckon it'd cost us an arm and a leg to get fixed up."

"Just leave it on the road?"

"Yeah. You want to keep it?"

"No."

"So there you go."

"Then what? What after this town? We hitch?"

"Seems like it. It's not so far from here. We'll manage it."

There wasn't much to collect from the car because we

had next to nothing with us. There were the two sleeping bags and the blanket and a little food.

I took the ugly porcelain elephant off the dashboard and put him in my backpack.

Cal said, "You should leave that here. Horrible thing. Better if it gets trashed with the car."

I shrugged. I said, "I like it."

"It's got wonky eyes."

"All the better to see you with."

We got into the cab of the truck.

There was a string of purple prayer beads hanging from the rearview mirror and on the end of the string was a yellow tassel and the beads swung violently when the truck was moving and tapped on the front windshield, and there were plastic cups with red-striped straws on the dashboard, balled-up paper burger bags, grease-stained, and a banana skin.

Scotch-taped beside the air vent was a photograph of two kids, a boy and a girl.

The driver said, "If you want my advice you call your insurance. They'll tow that away for you and get it off the roads."

"Sure, man. When we get to the next town."

"You make sure you do. That's a problem, abandoned vehicles. That's a real problem around here. I've been driving this road for years and I never saw anywhere like it for abandoned vehicles. Worse just these last few months, even. All sitting around on the side of the road rusting up."

"Really?"

"Honest to God. All over the place."

"Why here? Where do the people go?"

"Damned if I know."

He was right. On that stretch into town we saw two other empty cars on the side of the road. They were starting to rust over. One of them had the side door standing slightly open.

They seemed to be waiting for something.

The local town wasn't big, and it had that feel of a nearby border. The houses were low and flat and brick showed through falling uneven plaster.

The main street was quiet and people sat outside small cafes just staring. Walking sticks leaned against the legs of tables.

The driver said, "I'll drop you here then. There's a pizza place down at the end of the road. You can get a phone in there if yours won't work. For the insurance call. And you can get good pizza."

"Thanks."

He looked hesitant.

Then he put a hand on my arm. He said, a little self-consciously and speaking to Cal not to me, "Eidon's a long way to go tonight you know, man. A good long way.

Especially if you're catching a ride. You both all right for somewhere to sleep here tonight in case you need it? Got a bit of money for a room at an inn or something?"

Cal said, "We thought we'd just push it and make it down to the city."

"I'm telling you that's a long way. Little peanut here looks dead."

I said, "I'm fine."

The driver looked at me and blew out his cheeks and after a moment he said, "Look. I live here. I'm going to write down my address for you, there's a spare room at my place for the night if you need. It's not a big town here and it won't be easy to find somewhere last minute like this."

Cal and I looked at each other and I felt all of a sudden and inexplicably a little tearful.

It was because I was tired.

I said, "That's very kind."

"Welcome. I'm going now to drop the truck at the station. You both go and get yourselves some food and you can meet me at my address later if you need to. There'll be a bed for you there. Or a sofa anyway."

He got back in the front cab of the truck and drove off and left us standing in the middle of the street.

Cal looked at me. He said, "Do you want to do that?"

"We could sleep in a bed. I could have a shower."

"Not scared he's a serial killer?"

"I just want a shower."

"I guess after what we've been through, you can take care of yourself," he joked.

I stared. "Jesus, Cal. That's not funny."

"Sorry." After a moment he shrugged. "If you want to I'm happy to do it. I'm never going to complain about a bed."

Then he said, "You want to go and get something to eat before we meet him? I'll pay, my treat. Last leg of the voyage tomorrow."

I paused a moment.

I said, "OK. Yeah. Let's get something to eat."

We wandered down the street.

The late afternoon was hot and bright and the buildings seemed very white, white with dust, and there were small scrubby trees growing in special holes in the pavement and half of each trunk was painted white and the white paint had been made dirty and scummy, and each tree had an iron circle of fencing around it. At the end of the street a dog wandered slowly with its nose against the ground. It was long and lanky and dun-colored.

He said, "Look at this place."

"Somewhere from another time."

"Yeah."

There was a pizza restaurant opposite a supermarket which looked like it was the supermarket for the whole local area. It had old automatic doors in the front and they were slow-moving and every so often they jammed. We saw a big glass window with a display of old shop mannequins wearing swimming trunks and behind the mannequins there were cardboard palm trees even though the town here was far away from the ocean. A few people stood around in the parking lot talking with bags of shopping at their sides. A red-striped awning stuck out in front of the pizza restaurant with clustered zinc tables and chairs outside the front door, and there were two machines which dispensed plastic toys for a few coins, and laminated menus standing on the tables and old vinegar bottles and full ashtrays propping them up.

Inside a fan turned slowly and loudly.

The walls were covered with crucifixes and little signs with carefully hand-painted Bible quotes full of spelling errors.

I read one. It said:

**I KNOW THE PLANS I HAVE FOR YOU,
PLANS TO PROSPER AND NOT TO HAM YOU**

Cal and I looked at each other.

I said, "Let's sit outside."

"At least he doesn't want to ham us."

We ordered orange juice and beans with cheese and

chili peppers and garlic bread. At the table two cats wound slyly around the table legs searching for scraps.

I said, "Do you remember the tin can phones?"

He laughed. "What made you think of that?"

"I don't know."

It was something in the hot dry air, something about that baking white bright street and sitting away from it in the stippled shade of the awning and the orange juice and the cold metal tables and the lazy muted sounds of music on a stereo somewhere.

The tin can phones had been a stupid game we once played in our old apartment in San Padua just after we were married. There were these two kids playing up and down the hallway outside the door all afternoon and they had these food cans connected with string like two phones with a phone wire and they were running about up and down the corridor saying *hello, hello,* and Cal and I had opened the front door of the apartment to see what they were doing and found them reeling with laughter from whatever it was one of them had said to the other, and then that evening when I went out into the corridor again there had been the tin can phones lying on the floor.

The kids had gone and forgotten all about them.

And so I picked them up and took them inside to show Cal and we went down out of the apartment and walked onto the beach at night and stood under the streetlights and palm trees beside the sand in the hot damp, held in the sound of the ocean's rushing pump, talking in the tin can phones, stupid whispers, deep hot air, smell of sweat.

I have no idea what brought that back.

I had completely forgotten about it.

19

- - - - - - -

The trucker who had offered us a place to stay was called August Driver.

He lived in a little apartment above a liquor store which was open all night.

A neon sign hung above the shop door, pink and flickering and clouded with tiny flies. It was just beginning to switch on when we arrived in the gathering dark. It read:

24 HRS

The door for the apartments above the shop was to one side of the shop door and it was narrow and painted black and there was a slight smell of staleness around it. The buzzer hung a little askew, wires visible.

August Driver answered and said *come in* and led us up a little flight of stairs into his front room.

There was a door at one end leading out onto a tiny balcony with an iron railing around it, and the door was open and the linen curtains moved a little in the breeze.

In one corner beside the balcony door there was a bowl with cat food in it and it smelled strongly and the smell was in the apartment.

The far end of the room was the kitchen with a little round wooden table and two chairs, and the other end was the sitting area. There was an old mustard sofa with all the cushions worn bare and standing behind that was a tall lamp.

There were old black-and-white pictures on the walls, and some soccer prints too. Cal pointed to them. "You like soccer?"

"Yeah, yeah. Not to play. Just to follow, you know. Local team here does all right sometimes. We're doing well this year. You into soccer at all?"

"Not much."

August shrugged.

He said, "I've put out some blankets for you at the end of the sofa there. You can spread them out. It should be nice."

"Much appreciated."

"You want something to drink?" he said to me.

I smiled. "Sure."

"Whiskey? You like whiskey?"

He had some sort of sweet old spicy stuff at the back of a cupboard and the bottle was a little sticky and dusty. It looked as though it had been there for some time.

There was a picture of a stag or a moose on the front of it and it was standing in a meadow of wildflowers with a high mountain in the background and snow on top of the mountain. The colors were brash.

He said, "Had this lying around awhile, got it off a friend up north, might be for you, coming from near there."

When he lifted it out it left a ring of stain on the shelf.

He poured out three glasses. Its smell was of honey and something acrid which bit at the back of my throat and tasted the way it smelled and I wanted to spit it back out but didn't and smiled and said, "It's good," and hoped he didn't notice my eyes watering.

After a glass or two of whiskey he began to talk.

He seemed grateful for the chance and I wondered how much time he spent alone on those long tree-lined roads and in this dusty cat-food flat.

There had been the picture of the kids on the dashboard of the truck; the kids laughing; that little boy and girl. The picture had looked old.

It seemed that wherever they were now they were long gone out of his life.

August Driver told us how his grandfather used to drive a stagecoach when he had first moved to the country with his grandmother, and that the family name back then had been foreign, and people over here had struggled to pronounce it.

That family name was Krvntinekcz.

People in his native country had had trouble with it and it had nearly stopped August Driver's grandmother from marrying his grandfather, because she had said *how can I marry you when I wouldn't be able to say my own name* but she had married him anyway and so then that had been her name too. And when the family had moved across to start a new life in a new land August's grandfather had decided that here they would take a new name and because he was a driver of stagecoaches he had called himself Driver and his son had also been a driver of stagecoaches and a Driver, and now his son too—August.

He said, "I hate it. But with a name like that how could I do anything else? That's family."

Outside in the street someone was playing the harmonica quietly and it scratched at the late dark air.

August said, "Man, that sound. He's been sat outside playing that thing two nights now. Gets in my head."

He went over and shut the window and then there was only the slow hammering of the broken fan in the corner of the room and the buzzing of the flies on the cat food.

He said, "What was I talking about?"

"Family."

"Family. Oh. Yeah. I was going to say something else. I can't remember what."

"It'll come back."

"Yeah."

"When you're lying in bed trying to sleep."

"Yeah. Families. It was something about that. Oh well."

He lapsed into silence and sat at the wooden kitchen table staring ahead of himself, and his gaze seemed lost in something and far away. After a while he got up heavily and shambled over to the kitchen sink and swilled his glass out with water and without saying anything else went through into the bedroom and shut the door behind him.

I got up and spread out the blankets on the sofa and tucked them into the edges of the sofa cushions and made it up ready to sleep. Cal stood on the balcony with the glass door open smoking a joint and I could tell he was watching me. After he was finished he came and sat down at the kitchen table.

I was washing the whiskey glasses in the sink and I was humming that song again because it was lodged in my head and I couldn't get it out, *set out running but I'll take my time*, and all of a sudden Cal said, "This is what I wanted, you know."

His voice was slow and heavy. There was a sort of catch

in it that I wasn't used to and it was something childlike almost, sad.

I turned to him. I said, "What?"

He rolled the bottle cap across the top of the table with his finger. In the whitish light in the apartment I could see the lines in his face, just beginning, beginning to set.

In a few years' time he would look middle-aged.

He said, "This. You know." He nodded to the made-up sofa and to the sink and the apartment.

I said, "Me doing everything for you?"

"Come on. You know that's not what I meant." He paused for a moment and then said slowly, "That feeling, you know, like you've . . . landed somewhere. Like . . . this is it, like it's happened."

"What's happened?"

"I don't know. Life. Home. Something like that."

I stared at the water in the sink, slowly running down. An oily slick sat on its surface and moved about.

I said, "I don't know if you're ever going to find that, Cal."

"I think I did. First time around with you. Back then was just the wrong time."

"Cal—"

"Come on, Anne Marie."

"You don't know what you're saying."

He stared at me, and there was something in his eyes that was very hurt and lost and broken and tired.

He said, "Things have really changed for you then."

"Jesus Christ, I don't know. How am I supposed to know? You left, years ago, and I got on with some little life and got stuck in some shitty groove, and then you came back and broke all of that without even asking me and now you're saying and claiming all these things but what you think you want won't last five seconds down the line the moment you have it. I know that because I know myself and we're too alike in that, you and me. How am I supposed to know, Cal?"

He put a hand over his eyes.

In the corner the fan hammered away.

I said, "Is there a way to turn that off?"

He didn't answer. After a moment he got up and pulled the plug out of the wall.

He said, "Let's just go to bed."

We lay on the sofa and he put his arms around me and I lay with him holding me in the dark with the heavy smell of cat food and the room too hot and both of us pressed close on the sofa with no room to move and my body was broken by feelings that I didn't have a name for which were something like a sick yearning for what had been there in me a long time ago and wasn't there anymore.

From the next room there was the snoring of August Driver.

Long after Cal had fallen asleep I lay awake.

There were two things in my head that night.

One was the shape of Sandro Martin falling backward, and the other was my mother.

I remembered her long hair, which was yellow, playing with her long hair, and an impression of her perfume and her perfume was not a true memory because I had forgotten its real smell and only remembered that I had liked it, and it made me very sad that night in the hot crumbling town, the fact that I couldn't remember the smell of my mother's perfume.

20

- - - - - - -

We got a ride all the way down to Eidon Mountain with a man in a blue station wagon. The man's name was Wade Potts.

We stood on the main bypass outside the town the next morning after we had left the trucker, or I stood beside the road with my thumb out and Cal stayed back slightly but still close by, because we had found that people stopped more often when they saw a woman alone than when they saw a man and woman together.

And so the person who stopped for us was Wade Potts.

Wade Potts was going to the city of Eidon Mountain to stop the wedding of the woman he was in love with.

Wade had a black stretcher in his left earlobe and black

hair and his skin was tanned and his teeth were very white. I thought probably he had had them whitened.

He wore a denim shirt and two gold rings on his fingers and he played heavy metal on the radio.

His hair was gelled in spikes.

He talked a lot. Soon after we got in he told us about the girl he loved who would be marrying someone else the next morning in Eidon Mountain at the Orchid Imperial Hotel with a reception at the Orchid Imperial Casino. The casino and the hotel were affiliated. One was run by the father and one was run by the son. She was marrying the son and he was very wealthy. His name was Peter Simms. The girl's name was Luz Laney.

Luz Laney and Peter Simms had met at the San Padua branch of the Orchid Imperial Casino, where Luz went four nights a week because she had a gambling addiction.

Wade Potts had dumped her because of this addiction.

So Luz kept going to the casino and one night there she had met Peter who was handsome and rich and had paid for an expensive therapist who had helped her and together they had beaten back her addiction, which was an addiction to playing poker, and he had bought her a nice black dress and introduced her to his father and told the old man they were getting married, and Luz in a moment of impulse had sent a wedding invite—white and red with a dove on the top—to her ex Wade Potts, who had received it and remembered that he loved her and was now on his way steaming down the long highway between San Padua and Eidon Mountain, over the scrubby land, to go and tell her so.

And that was where he had picked us up.

He said, "It's moments like that that show you what's meaningful in life, you know? I got that envelope and it was just like a kick in the head."

Cal said, "We know. We're married."

I said, "We were married."

"We're still married."

I elbowed him in the ribs.

Wade Potts kept talking. He had barely noticed.

He was saying, "Luz, she's got these dogs, fancy dogs, you know? Awful things cost a fortune. Cost a fortune. Just to buy one, you know? Then there's all the shit they need. Combs, little jackets, dog treats, stuff like that—"

"Yeah."

"You got dogs?"

"No."

"Shit, man. You're lucky. Horrible things. Horrible. They're what-do-you-call-it, Pomeranian, that's it— Pomeranian. Come with, like, certificates and a family tree and stuff because they're purebreds. She's got this one. Domino. Bites the shit out of my ankles every time it sees me."

There was a small plastic woman in a bikini on the dashboard and the top half of her body was designed to wobble with the motion of the car. Her top half went one way and her bottom half the other. It was meant to look like she was dancing.

Her arms were in the air.

I watched her, hypnotized by the rhythm of her movements, while Wade Potts talked. Out of the car window we were passing under red cliffs which towered up above us, rough slabs running deep with a branched lacework of cracks, burnt amber and streaked brown and sand yellow, and here and there little shrubs clinging onto ledges in the rock, and along the top, high above us, a hanging fringe, just visible, of a few twisted branches growing up in the summit. The road wound along underneath it all, stretching ahead.

Wade said, "It gets like this now most of the way to Eidon. All cliff land like this, all crags. We're out of the forests here. You know the area around the city much?"

Cal said, "I was there a little while a few years ago."

I said, "My mother was from Eidon City. I was born there. We moved away when I was a year old."

Cal looked at me quickly.

I said, "You'd forgotten that, hadn't you?"

"No."

"Yes you had."

My mother and I had lived together until I was fifteen. She had told me stories about growing up in the city which was named after the mountain standing over it.

She had lived there with her father who had been an artist, because it was a place where lots of artists moved to go and paint the mountains and watch morning light on the cliffs.

He had not been a good artist, viewed from a point of view of financial success.

In fact, viewed from a point of view of financial success, he had been a mediocre to bad artist. He'd made a modicum of money and had been able to afford food for himself and my mother but nothing over and above that.

He had not achieved anything more or less than their survival.

He made art prints of images of different types of fruits and vegetables cut in half, in all kinds of colors. They were sold to people who wanted them for offices and hotel rooms and the foyers of library buildings, but he never managed to sell very many.

My mother had left when she was quite young. She had gone north to San Padua when she was eighteen and there she had worked first as a waitress and then as a barmaid and then one evening walking on the beach she had met my father.

His name was Jim Daws.

They never married. They told each other they didn't want to. Secretly I think she had wanted to be married.

When she was twenty-four or so I was born and she named me after a song and then the year after that my father disappeared and was never seen or heard of by either of us again, although it was thought that he had run away with the girl who lived in the apartment below them at the time and who was called Sheena Spinks, at least it was thought by my mother and her friends.

She never talked to me about my father.

I never found it possible to work out whether or not she missed him.

There were a lot of things about her I never found it possible to work out.

At home she had sometimes been vague and at other times drifting and she would go about the house and off to work and look always a little lost, a little bemused.

Most of the time in the evenings she kept on the blue uniform she had worn in the office during the day. That uniform had a white collar and a little daisy stitched on the pocket and the daisy was also blue on a blue background.

She had a set of those uniforms, and once a week she sat up ironing them all for the week ahead and folding them and putting them into the cupboard in the hallway.

And I used to sit on the sofa and watch her while she ironed, watch her face which became distant with concentration.

I remember one time she burned her hand on the iron. I heard it burn, a crisp sizzle.

And she didn't do anything. She didn't jerk her hand away, she didn't yell.

She stood there and looked down at her hand and the long red mark starting to appear there, and she and I both watched it come up on her skin.

And I remember I said *doesn't it hurt?*

And she said *no*.

She would put those classic guitar records on after I had gone to bed and play them in the living room. My bedroom was the next along and the two rooms shared a wall, and I would fall asleep to the faint sounds of the music, and to other sounds which were small and difficult to place, tiny quiet scuffs of movement, and I would imagine my mother, dancing alone in the dark room to the old sad music.

I never went in.

I have no idea if she was really dancing.

Some nights when I was lying in bed I'd hear the soft click of the bedroom door handle and quiet footsteps across the carpet of the floor and the sound of her breathing, and feel the sagging of the mattress beside my head as she sat down. She would stroke my hair, carefully, slowly, and I would lie in the fuzzed dark at the edge of sleep, a red-tinted dark behind my eyes, in a warm ball curled under the covers, eyes closed, her soft breath the rhythm of an ocean.

One day when I was fifteen she was walking on the beach promenade, and sometimes down on the beach there were these horses who gave rides for tourists, and they wore blankets on their backs and they had ribbons in their hair, and one of them in a red blanket and red ribbons had seen a kite on the beach which had just been released by a kid who was flying it and so this horse reared up in fright all of a sudden and bucked and kicked, and kicked my mother who was walking behind it to cross the road and who had been afraid of horses her whole life.

She lay in a hospital bed for a week.

Her heart was beating but her brain was gone.

I sat on this chair during visitors' hours and stared at the wall and ate bad hospital food, and sometimes the nurses came around to check on me and said *tell us if you need anything*. Every evening my aunt and uncle came to pick me up and I slept in the spare bedroom of their house.

One night there was a phone call from the hospital and my aunt took it. She was in the front hallway of the house and I was sitting behind her on the stairs. After a moment she turned around and saw me sitting there.

Her face crumpled and she said, "I'm sorry, sweetheart, oh God, I'm sorry."

And that was when the emptiness started.

Afterward I remember standing alone in a small front room and there were piles of cardboard boxes in front of me with brown tape on them. My mother's name was written on the top in marker pen. It had been written by the removal men and they had spelled it wrong the first few times and then crossed out the misspellings so that her name was now under stacked scribbles.

They were fumbling, awkward. They said *sorry, sorry,* and I said *it's all right.*

I was there with Tricia and my aunt and uncle, which made up a lot of people in the small room, and it was the middle of summer and the curtains were drawn and so the room was horribly hot and red. After a while the others went outside. They said they would give me a moment and I was glad they had gone because I barely knew them and I wanted them out.

And so I stood alone and all around me were boxes with our things in them and they were all taped shut and stood there bland and meek and it somehow made me angry, the meekness, the stacked boxes waiting by the door, waiting in a row, and I wanted to break them and kick them and scream wordless.

Instead I went through to my mother's bedroom and there was the dressing table which hadn't been packed up yet and there was a bottle of perfume in the middle of it which was the perfume that she liked to wear. The bottle was made of clouded glass with roses on it, and the lid was in the shape of a dove.

I picked it up and threw it on the floor and it smashed. A pool of liquid soaked darkly into the edge of the rug and made the air acrid.

Anyway.

That was the last time I was in my mother's house.

Once when I was still in school about a year after it happened someone said to me *you never talk about her*.

And I said *I don't know what to say.*

21

- - - - - - -

Eidon Mountain rose up suddenly as we came around a bend, and the orange cliffs fell away and became a wide valley plain ringed by red mountains, steep and abrupt and obscured by a haze in the distance, small low clouds clinging around their bases.

Through the middle of the red floodplain ran a river, a slim line in the sun. It showed black on the valley floor and the city sprawled around its length, winking with small shards of light reflecting off the glass of apartment buildings which sat oddly shrunken beneath the mountains.

Out to the west beyond the edges of the city were flat slabbed rows of solar panels, enormous, blunt, bright.

These solar panels were famous for being the largest in the country.

Power lines ran back from them and powered all of the city, and other lines ran underground and went out through the mountains and farther, to other cities and other towns. So this place sat out in the dry heat, a big shiny plate collecting sunlight, all this sunlight pooling in and spilling in on those plates, and then those plates and their atoms soaked up more and more of that sun and the little electrons buzzing around those atoms got more and more of that energy and as they got more and more of that energy they spun faster and eventually careened off on their own little paths, zipped off, little bundles of negative charge, and all sped in one great enthusiastic wave in search of something positive and thus made an electric current. And that electric current went speeding along tubes that branched and branched and ultimately became the movement of a hairdryer fan or the chatter of a TV screen.

We wound down toward the city.

The lower we got into the valley the hotter it got in the little car.

Wade Potts rolled up the windows and turned on the air conditioning, and cold air which smelled of plastic began to move about.

The hula girl on the dashboard swung violently.

Cal said, "Jesus. This place holds the heat."

And Wade Potts laughed and said, "You should come here in the middle of summer."

The road widened into a six-lane highway and filled up with cars and became a choked-up tide of slow-moving traffic. Horns blared and Wade blared his. It was very loud.

He said, "When in Rome."

I looked out of the window.

Around us cars crawled on toward the city.

22

We left Wade Potts at four in the afternoon in the parking lot of the Orchid Imperial Hotel, which was where he parked his car.

The hotel was built to look like an Arabian palace.

Cal and I stood beside the hibiscus flowers and watched Wade Potts walk in through the revolving doors and disappear.

I said, "Do you think she'll go with him?"

Cal shrugged. He said, "Probably already married to the other guy by now."

"Funny that we'll never know."

"Is it?"

We began walking. To our left and to our right there

stretched the long thoroughfare of the main road into the center of the city.

Shop fronts and hotel fronts and restaurant fronts in flat-roofed buildings opened off it.

Up above us the sky was wide and yellow and ripening.

Cal said, "Where do you want to go? New city. We have an evening."

I hesitated for a moment and looked about.

On the other side of the road opposite us there was a sign which said MUNICIPAL ARBORETUM.

"There," I said pointing to the sign. "Let's go there."

Cal laughed. "You want to go and see the trees?"

"You don't have to come."

"No—no. I want to."

The arboretum gates were a little way down the road. They were black and old and the paint was falling off them and this paint was crusted and lumped because somebody had painted over rust.

The gates stood partially open and along the ground at their base were long deep score marks in the concrete where they had been dragged over and over again.

There was nobody else there.

A long avenue of cedars led away from us and under their branches it was dark and already almost night and it smelled of damp and green sap cooking and there were the first brittle stirrings of cicadas and the shifting of leaves.

Behind us evening fell over the thoroughfare and there was the movement of cars and the smell of gasoline, dying light on metal.

We walked in under the trees.

Cal took my hand in his and I looked down sharply and he glanced at me and I thought about all the nights in that ugly old apartment, that darkness, those broken walls heavy with mold and the sound of the sirens outside and the flash of blue lights on the ceilings in the dark and the other sounds coming through the walls, other people spreading about the little noises of their lives which soaked into the walls and came to me in the dark, and then nights and nights alone with some nondescript darkness of a body beside me, the sound of the breathing of another person, an unknown, two lives parked up side by side for one night and one night only, a brief overlapping of realities, a momentary collision before blundering separately off again, both reeling headlong into separate confusions, separate strings of light and sound, all the time with the aching idea of him, of Cal, which sat at the back of my brain and which I tried not to let myself look at ever but which nevertheless I sometimes did, which I sometimes let myself take out and pore over to torture my brain with the searing pain of it, all the time knowing that he would never come back to me and he would never try to take my hand the way he had done now.

And he didn't understand, that was the thing, he thought he did but he didn't.

Behind us there was the chinking of metal.

I looked back.

Cal said, "They're closing the park. Come on. Let's go and try to find somewhere for the night."

"Cal."

"Yeah."

I shrugged, looked away. "Doesn't matter. It's nothing."

"What is it? You've gone distant on me. You look distant."

"No. It's all right."

"If something's up you have to tell me. I can't read your mind, Anne Marie."

"I know. I don't want you to."

We left the park as the warden was closing the gates for the evening and he pulled them shut behind us and they screamed on the concrete. It made the hairs on my arms stand up.

23

- - - - - -

Down a small side street there was a little place offering
rooms.

It was called Royal Desert Inn and Bar. The name was
written on a sign above the door and the letters were neon
green and pink but some of them didn't work and flick-
ered on and off, so that sometimes the sign said ROYAL
DE ER INN AND BAR.

The bar was in evidence.

It was built across the main front of the building, tables
and stools spilling over into the little alley, and there was
a woman standing behind the bar under the dirty yellow
light and she had bright dyed red hair which looked odd
in the odd chemical lighting. It was hard to tell how old

she was. Her body looked young but her face was haggard in the shadows. In her ears there were large rings.

She was talking to a man who leaned on the bar. Every now and again they stopped and stared together at the people around them.

Others sat on stools at the little outside tables, or they stood in the alley and pulled at cigarettes and talked, and the air was thick with smoke and its hazy swirls were picked out by the neon.

Cal asked and the woman at the bar pointed us through a side door.

She said, "Reception's in there."

Then she said, "Have a nice night."

Through the door there was a small room and the walls were painted dark red and they were stained with squashed mosquitoes. In one corner a big dark plant stood with heavy leaves, ugly, obtrusive, and there was a desk which took up a lot of room and behind the desk on the wall was a calendar. It was a joke calendar. It showed three men posing in kilts and they were topless and muscular and tanned and behind them rolled the soft green of some hilly countryside on the other side of the world.

Under that were rows and rows of sticky notes and on the sticky notes was crass rounded handwriting, phone numbers I think, and names and things like that.

There was a girl behind the desk.

She smoked a cigarette and the end of the cigarette was crumbling ash, a fat wad of crumbling ash hanging on the glowing end and quivering with the movement of her hand as she held it there slightly away from her to blow a long stream of smoke in the other direction. And there was a can on the countertop, a beer can, which had been cut open and folded and bent so that it could be used as an ashtray. And the girl tapped the cigarette on the side of the can and the wad of ash fell off and landed on the ash that was already in there. This girl had dark hair and it was cut into a bob in line with her chin. She wore a pink shirt. On the front of the shirt was black writing.

It said, *Cherry Bomb.*

The girl stared belligerently.

Cal said, "You have a room free for the night?"

She snorted. "We always have rooms free."

"A double. One night."

Her left eyebrow twitched and she stared at us and drew dolefully at the cigarette. Then she said, "Yeah," and reached under the desk and brought out a paper.

"Fill this in. That's yours. Then fill this in. That's ours."

She dropped a key on the form. "Room six. It's the second floor along the hall. Green door." Upstairs the corridor smelled strongly of insect repellent, and then once we had unlocked the door and gone inside, room 6 smelled the same.

I said, "Let's open a window."

And Cal said, "Probably not a good idea here."

I heard him fumbling along the wall for a light switch.

He said, "Jesus. Does this dump not have lights?"

I went over to the bed and turned on the bedside lamp.

Cal's face looked white and worn in the light.

On the bedside table was a little porcelain statuette of a spaniel dog. It was white and it had gold ears and a gold collar and the gold had rubbed off in patches and its eyes bulged and they pointed in slightly different directions.

I nodded at it. I said, "One eye to watch you, one to watch me."

He scoffed.

Outside in the street there was the sound of breaking glass.

Someone shouted loudly and then there was silence, then a woman's screeched laugh.

Cal lay down on the bed and I came over and lay down beside him and he put his arms around me and for a while it felt only good and not confusing to have him do that, for a moment it was only sensation.

He leaned over me and turned off the bedside lamp.

In the dark there was a shape on the opposite wall.

I stared at it.

I said, quietly, "Cal."

He said, "Yes."

I felt his hand. He was stroking my hair. He said, "I think I know. But you can't think about it. You said it yourself. Don't think about it."

I said, "It sometimes comes into my head when I'm trying to sleep."

"I know."

"What the alley looked like."

"It didn't look like anything. It was dark."

"I know. But in my head I change it. When I remember. It's hard to think how it really was. I think I make up being able to see more than I actually did."

His hand stroked my hair.

After a moment I said, "Do you think about it?"

"Yes. Of course." His voice was flat. "It doesn't take it back. You can think about it for a thousand years but it doesn't take it back. It was just what happened. Better him than us."

Then he said, "Go to sleep, Anne Marie."

His hand on my hair felt somehow unsettling.

It wasn't something he had done for a long time, even when we were married, I think by that time he had more or less already stopped doing it. Strange that I hadn't thought it was wrong at the time. Strange that I hadn't second-guessed it.

After we were married we rented an apartment in a big old pink townhouse one block away from the ocean. The building was tumbling down into the street like all the other buildings in that area and so it always had scaffolding on its front face to keep it held up and that meant that you could climb out of any of the front windows and sit on the wooden boards of the scaffolding at night and listen to the sea with the hot breeze on your face.

And I was living there with Cal, of course, although at that time things were already going bad.

One night I found a message from another woman on his phone.

I didn't know who she was; I didn't recognize the name. Cal had never spoken about her. I found it by accident because I had picked up his phone to see the time and there it was on the screen.

And I had gone straight through to the bedroom, lain on the bed with my back to the door looking at the dark wall with my eyes open. There was this ugly old stucco stuff on the walls and it made patterns in the light coming through the door from the far hallway, and I touched it with my finger and I remember being surprised that it was cold.

Cal had woken me up later that night moving around in the room.

He made small noises when he tripped over things.

I was afraid of his reaction and afraid of losing him, and so I never told him I had seen that message.

He never knew I knew.

The glowing clock face under the TV on the wall said five o'clock in the morning.

I had woken abruptly and at first I thought that there must have been some sound or something to wake me, but I lay still and there was nothing. Cal was burning hot beside me and his arm was pressed against mine. His body twitched a little with dreaming.

Gently I moved away from him toward the edge of the bed. He rolled over and I stopped, and then he settled back and I moved again. I sat with my feet planted on the floor and looked at him sleeping.

I knew it was time to go.

I didn't know how long I had known that for, without admitting it. Some time anyway.

I had felt it and I hadn't wanted to look at it but I had known that sooner or later I would have to.

This way round was better.

I felt about on the floor for my backpack and my hands moved over it and I picked it up and put it on.

I was still wearing all my clothes.

The door of the room creaked a little when I opened it and a line of light came in from the corridor, and grew, and became a wedge with the opening of the door. I stood for a moment in the doorway and looked back in at the room. It was full of the heavy sounds of Cal's breathing.

I closed the door quietly behind me and walked down the corridor to the stairwell.

24

- - - - - - -

There was nobody in the little booth of the reception.

The room stood empty and quiet in the pinkish light from a corner lamp, the bar shut up.

Outside the first shade of pale was showing above the horizon.

A man was half lying against the wall in the street and when he saw me come out of the door he rolled toward me and said something in a slurred voice and I turned away and began to walk quickly toward the light of the main street where there were cars, those odd early-morning cars, early risers, the first commuters, and where soon there would be people and the opening of bakeries and maybe I could get a little food.

In my head I wrote, over and over, the first few lines of a letter which was a letter to Cal. Began it and then stopped.

There wouldn't have been any point.

Out on the main street the lights made the beginning of the dawn go away, made it impossible to see.

A corner shop was taking a delivery from the open back of a truck and two men pushed at a tall cage-like cart and it rattled on concrete and they swore and pulled at it when it hit the curb, and there was the quiet chinking of the bottles which sat in the cage of the cart in cardboard boxes.

A white light was on in the window of the little shop.

One of the men was staring at me and he said something to the other and they both turned and looked at me for a long time with hard looks and my spine tingled and I turned and began to walk quickly away from them in the other direction.

I thought, A cafe, I need some service place to sit quiet and warm and safe while the sun comes up and then I can know where I'm going.

A red car pulled up beside me and a man leaned out of the window.

He said, "Need a place to sleep, sweet?"

He had graying hair and his nose disfigured his face.

I kept walking.

For a while the car crawled along behind me and every now and again he would call something out.

Eventually he snickered and I heard the acceleration of the engine as he drove past me and away.

I tried to imagine my mother living here in this city and when I imagined my mother as my age I imagined her as me, which happened because it was impossible for me to imagine her as herself.

I pictured her walking down a lightening road.

There was a gas station on the corner of the main street and it had a forecourt lit up with white and blue lights, which were fixed blockish on cables overhead.

Inside there was a cafeteria and it was open and there were long plastic tables and I bought a coffee and sat down at one.

I wondered whether Cal would try to find me.

I didn't see how he would be able to.

Maybe he had woken up early the way he sometimes did, and so maybe he would already know by now that I had gone.

He might think in the beginning that I had just gone down to the front room of the inn or something. He would lie there for a while and I thought he would try to come up with reasons and explanations for where I might be, and then after a while he would realize that I had gone and that I wasn't coming back at least in his foreseeable future and that I had left him.

That would be new to him.

I wondered if my absence would destroy him.

I thought it wouldn't.

He was not someone who could ever relinquish himself enough for a word as powerful as *destruction*.

I wondered where I thought I was going to go, because it couldn't be San Padua now, I couldn't go back there.

A car pulled up on the forecourt and a man got out and went into the shop next door and I heard the automatic doors when he came in, and then a moment later he walked back across the forecourt. In his arms there were two packets of potato chips and two bottles of water.

A small face was in the passenger seat of the car. I saw her as he drove away past the window, a little girl, eating a bag of potato chips.

The father and the girl looked tired.

And for a moment I felt it too, an ache to be tired and driving in the car in the early morning with a father, who was also tired, both of us eating potato chips which smelled of rich dog food, and drinking cold bottled water.

I stared at the tabletop.

It had a rough surface and there were small spots of gray on it which were the pattern on the plastic.

It was the same as the tabletops that had been in my

school. For part of my life I had looked at tabletops like them and drawn on them. I had liked drawing fish. I was good at it. There weren't many things I could draw well from my imagination but for some reason I used to draw those fish all the time over everything and I had a sort of template of steps that I followed in my head of the exact way in which they had to be drawn.

In school my teachers told me I was clever. A teacher called Mrs. Romero had taken a special interest in me. She had worn these purple reading glasses and her hair had been dyed blond and she was in her fifties, late fifties, something like that, so presumably under the dye it was gray.

She had a small plastic man sitting on her desk.

The man was yellow and he was holding a plastic sign.

The sign said:

MAKE TODAY ANOTHER SUNNY DAY!

I had stared at that sign every morning for two years.

I breathed out.

Sooner or later I was going to have to decide where to go.

25

"Hello?"

"Hi, Tricia."

"Anne Marie?"

"Yeah."

"Jesus, it's five-thirty in the morning. You woke me. Where are you?"

"I'm in Eidon."

"What? You're there?"

"Yeah."

"Just a minute."

There was shouting at the other end of the line as Tricia told the kids to pipe down.

Then Tricia said, "Sorry."

"No, it's fine."

"What's going on? Are you all right, is everything OK?"

I paused. I said, "I think I might need to come and stay with you for a little while."

"Of course—of course, whatever you need. Are you safe? I can come and get you—Josh can come and get you with the car—"

"No. No, it's fine, I can come to your place. I'll get a metro out."

"You sure?"

"Yeah."

"Where are you now?"

"A gas station. It says West Avenue Services. On the edge of the city. There's a metro station at the end of the street, I passed it when I came here."

"Do you have any money?"

"Enough for a ticket I think."

"You call me if anything goes wrong, all right? Just call me. The stop is Cicada Street. You get off there and I'll be waiting for you."

"Thank you, Tricia."

"I'll see you soon."

"Yeah."

I sat in the big empty cafeteria and cars and people began to arrive.

New workers came in and changed shifts with the people who were at the gas station already and they wore the same uniform which was a white shirt with a logo on the pocket and the woman who now stood behind the counter wore the same white paper hat as the man who had left and when she arrived the two of them barely said a word to each other and just changed places and then she stood in his same position and he walked out across the cafeteria and through the automatic doors and began to cross the forecourt.

He walked slowly, shoulders hunched over.

And outside the window cars began to go by on the roads and people began to walk past on the pavement beyond the forecourt.

Cal would have woken up by now.

At this moment maybe he was waiting for me in the inn. If he was doing that then he would be sitting on the end of the bed. He would be biting his nails.

He was a nail biter in uncertain situations.

I tried to picture what his expression would be.

I couldn't.

I couldn't even picture his face.

I tried to think of how he might be feeling and I had no idea because I had no idea what I was for him.

So he would either be sitting on that bed in that room in that inn waiting for me, or he would already have left by now, and then I couldn't picture anything past that.

Maybe he was on a bus.

Maybe he was looking out of a window and maybe meeting the eye of a pretty girl sitting across the aisle from him, or maybe not, maybe he was just looking out of the window at the city going by and maybe in this bus he had already gone past me in this gas station cafeteria where I was sitting.

Jesus.

I have to move, I thought, I have to make myself move, and my body felt heavy.

I have to, I have to, and I stood and my legs were dead from sitting cramped on them for so long.

I walked out of the cafeteria and across the forecourt and onto the street.

It was maybe about six o'clock and the early air smelled cold.

Up in the middle of the sky was the last star of the night.

I felt bleached out, hollow.

At the far end of the street were the first seeps of pale yellow and the slivered edge of the sun, and as I watched it rose up higher.

The sky burst into pink and then red and orange ripped out wide across the clouds, whipped and wheeling with the high spiraling of early birds, and everything except them was still.

Sunrise stretched out above me in hugeness and the

air was full of color and underneath it I was a tiny upright shape.

The last moments of the night died.

I walked alone down an early-morning street toward the station.

Acknowledgments

To my incredible editors, Parisa Ebrahimi and Kate Harvey, and my wonderful agent, Emma Paterson: you have been such friends and guides throughout this process and it has been a pleasure to work with you.

Thank you for all that you do.

I am also so grateful to everyone in the teams at Penguin Random House and Aitken Alexander Associates who've had a hand in this book. It would not have been possible without you and I am humbled by the unfailing support you give.

PHOTO: JOEL FULLWOOD

AILSA MCFARLANE was born in 1997 in Seattle, Washington, and grew up in Snowdonia in the United Kingdom. After leaving school, she studied veterinary science before dropping out to travel the United States and Europe by road. *Highway Blue* is her first novel.